WEDLOCK

MARK SPENCER

Watermark Press, Inc.
149 N. Broadway
Wichita, Kansas 67202

Library of Congress Cataloging-in-Publication Data

Spencer, Mark, 1956-
  Wedlock: two novellas.

  *Contents: Things to Come — Wedlock — Vicki's Place — Samson — Deja
vu.*
  I. Title.
PS3569.P4536W44   1988   *813'.54*   *88-33896*
  ISBN 0-922820-02-3

Cover Art: Kirsten Johnson
Design: Kirsten Johnson
Production: Cynthia Mines, John Hiebert

First Edition

For Diana

ACKNOWLEDGMENTS

In the short novel "Wedlock," some brief passages appeared in different forms in short stories published in *Gambit Magazine*, *Beloit Fiction Journal*, and *The Laurel Review*.

Brief portions of "Samson" appeared in very different forms in a story published in *The Florida Review*.

"Things to Come" first appeared in *Z Miscellaneous*.

CONTENTS

WEDLOCK

THINGS TO COME

My wife of four months is on the phone, talking to the post office. "I want to mail a body. . . ." She pauses, sticks out her tongue, and crosses her eyes to indicate to me that the person on the other end is a moron. No, it's just the body of my cat—" While she listens, tears well up in her eyes. She nods a couple of times, her shoulders hunched up close to her ears, before saying, "Okay. Thank you. Good bye."

She's sitting in the overstuffed chair next to the end table where the phone is, the cat on her lap. Jerry is not dead yet, but the vet gives him only a day or two.

Bev wouldn't let the vet put Jerry to sleep. She wants him to die at home, in her arms, then mail his body to her parents in Wisconsin so that he can be put to rest among her mother's chrysanthemums in the back yard. Bev's known the cat a dozen years longer than she's known me.

"What did they say?" I ask.

"The people at the post office are as stupid as everybody else in this town." There are pink splotches on her face. She gets them when she's nervous or upset. In our wedding pictures she has them. She wipes her eyes with the back of her hand and strokes Jerry with the other. "Maybe I should call UPS."

"What did the people at the post office say?"

"I don't want Jerry to die."

"I know."

"You're going to have to give me a tranquilizer when it happens. You know that, don't you?"

"Yes."

"I can't believe you can't do something for him."

"The vet can't help him. Why should I be able to?"

"You're a real doctor. You're supposed to be better than a veterinarian."

"You think I save all the people I take care of?"

Bev looks at me as though I just told her something she never knew.

I get up from my chair and look out the front window. The houses across the street are old and small, like ours. I'm in my first year of residency, and Bev and I don't have much money.

Three little boys are sitting on the curb in front of our house, each with a shovel. They live next door and have asked about Jerry because they've seen Bev taking him to the vet. They know he's dying, and they've offered to bury him for us.

"Are they still there?" Bev asks.

"Sure. Burying the cat will probably be the highlight of their week."

"I'm not letting them bury him. He's not going to be buried in Texas. He's going to be buried in Wisconsin if I have to take him there myself. He is a Wisconsin cat."

"You want a Tylenol Three?"

"You know Tylenol Three makes me think Satan's after me."

"Sorry."

"You can tell those little creatures to put their shovels away."

"Will the post office mail Jerry?"

"God, I need a drink." She gets up, still holding the cat. He's a full-blooded Siamese with a dark brown coat that used to be thick and glossy. Now there are spots where fur has fallen out. His breath is raspy, and sometimes he coughs up blood.

I hear the cabinets in the kitchen banging and glasses clinking. Bev's getting some more vodka. She's grown very fond of vodka. She mutters something sweet to Jerry.

I holler, "You know humans can catch things from cats, and you've got him in there in the kitchen."

She screams. And I run to her.

"Another cricket," she says. "It was about a foot long." The cat's slung over Bev's shoulder like a mangy fur piece.

I go back to the living room. Bev is saying, "I thought that spray was supposed to kill them. The whole damn house is full of crickets."

"There are a lot of bugs in Texas. I've told you before. We're lucky we got rid of the roaches and spiders."

A cabinet bangs in the kitchen.

I'm looking out the window at the kids with their shovels, and I think about last night. About one a.m. two teenage girls were brought into the E.R. They'd been tooling around in a little Chevette. Friday night and all. They were probably looking for soldiers; that's what young girls around here do since there's an army base nearby. A drunk private ran them off the road and they rolled. The paramedics brought them in all messed up. I didn't know where to start. Some old nurse yelled orders. Then a couple of surgeons showed up. I did what I was told.

By three a.m. everything was quiet—as I said, they were really messed up—and I went into the doctor's lounge. The TV was on, but nobody was in there. I went over to a window and looked out at the dark parking lot. The lounge was dark, too, except for the TV. The old movie *Things to Come* was on. Years and years passed, and it was one war after another, and the whole world went to hell.

Bev says, "There was a cricket in the bathroom last night. The biggest, blackest thing I've ever seen." The cat starts coughing, and I turn around in time to see Bev drop her glass. "He's spitting up on me!"

I take Jerry so that Bev can go change, and I sit down and stroke him. He stops coughing and even purrs a little.

"I can't take any more." Bev is standing in the doorway, bare chested and holding a clean blouse.

"Any more what?"

"Anything. Do you think Jerry could have caught a disease from a bug?"

"He's thirteen years old. That's what's wrong with him."

Bev's breasts are firm and high, but her face is splotched and twisted up. "You don't think those little creatures next door gave him something, do you?"

"Why do you think those little kids are such juvenile delinquents?"

"Look at their parents."

"What about them?"

"Their mother must weigh two hundred pounds, and she dresses like Miss Polyester of 1988."

"Come off it."

"My God, it's September, and they've got Christmas lights all over their house. Those big, old-fashioned kind of lights. What kind of people leave Christmas lights on their house all year?"

I glare at her. Then she turns and walks away. Her breasts bounce. One of the RNs on night shift is short and buxom. She keeps catching me looking at her. She just smiles, and so far we've pretended nothing is happening, or going to.

I lay the cat on the carpet and pat his head, and I go to the window again. The boys are digging in our front yard. They're digging a hole big enough for two people.

I holler to Bev, "Hey, what did the post office say?"

She doesn't answer. She's in the kitchen again, banging cabinets and clinking glasses. I look at Jerry. He's stretched out, and he's not moving.

"Honey," I say.

"Leave me alone," she says.

WEDLOCK

ONE

O ne spring morning when Pamela is feeling opti-
mistic about having a good day (after all, good
things are bound to happen *some*time), her
mother calls to tell her Lon's father has died.

"It was in the paper yesterday, but I knew you were
workin', and I didn't want to bother you late last night."

Pamela divorced Lon nearly six years ago. "So what
about it?"

There's silence. Then her mother says, "I thought you'd
want to know. I thought you liked Lon's dad."

Pamela doesn't say anything for a moment. Now she
feels guilty, and her day is ruined for sure. "Yeah, I liked
him. It's just it's been years since I saw him."

"He was a good man."

"I know."

"He had a hard time after his wife passed away."

"Mom, I gotta get ready for work."

"Okay. I'm sorry I took up your time. I just thought
you'd want to know since you-know-who will be coming
back from wherever he is. His dad didn't have anybody

else to leave that farm to."

"I didn't hear you, Mom, cause I don't want to know or think about it."

"I hear that farm got real run-down."

"Okay. Bye."

"You still havin' that weird dream about you and Lon?"

"No. Bye." Pamela hangs up.

A couple of years ago Pamela told her mother about the dream she keeps having—that she's been having ever since about two years after she divorced Lon. She needed to tell somebody, but telling Mom was a mistake because Mom keeps reminding her about it just when Pamela's managed to put it out of her head.

She goes into the bathroom and starts putting on makeup, getting ready to go to work at the McDonald's in Peebles. She figures restaurant work is all she can do. The mobile-home park she lives in is just outside of West Union, but West Union doesn't have a McDonald's, just Jack's Eats; and Jack and his wife, Louise, run the place by themselves. Pamela wouldn't want to work there anyway. The last time she ate there she got a piece of bread half covered with mold.

Bobby, her second husband, is in the spare bedroom of their trailer, fooling with his toys. She doesn't know what he does in there with them. He hasn't had a job for a year and a half, but he tells people he's a dealer in rare, collectable toys. For a few months, after he got laid off from the feed mill, he applied for a job every once in a while, but nothing ever came of it. He spent most of his time watching TV; around eleven every night, he'd make a run to the Taco Bell in Peebles because, he said, he had a craving for burritos. This was his routine.

Now he spends a lot of his time driving all over southern Ohio and northern Kentucky, buying toys at garage sales and flea markets. He has dozens of rusty, beat-up tricycles, trucks, cars, airplanes, spaceships, and wagons.

At first, Pamela didn't believe people actually collected

old toys and spent a lot of money on them. Then she remembered her aunt who had hundreds of little spoons with state slogans and seals on them and the names of tourist attractions like Yellowstone Park, the Everglades, and Disney World (that one had a handle shaped like Mickey Mouse). Her aunt ordered the spoons from a catalogue. And there was Pamela's sixty-year-old cousin who collected baseball cards. He had a Hank Aaron rookie card he claimed he paid a hundred dollars for. People collected *anything*, Pamela realized. Bobby told her he knew a guy who had a collection of over three thousand beer cans.

Every other day or so, Bobby tells Pamela he figures he has around ten thousand dollars' worth of toys, which he's spent only four hundred dollars on.

But so far he hasn't sold anything. Once, he took several toys to Cincinnati to see whether a dealer there wanted to buy some of them, but he brought them all home. Pamela didn't ask what happened, and he didn't say. For a week he didn't go to any flea markets or garage sales, just watched game shows and cartoons on TV and read *True Crime* magazines. Then one afternoon he went out and came back with a rusty tricycle that had a great big front wheel and said, "God Jesus, Pam, can you believe I paid only forty dollars for this? This thing's worth ten times that much. Got it from an old woman that's movin' to an old folks home. She didn't know nothin'."

Pamela was mixing pancake batter for supper and trying to figure out in her head how many hours she had to work at McDonald's to make forty dollars.

On her way to work in her '74 Maverick, Pamela can't help thinking about the dream. She and Lon are making love, and at first Lon has his torso arched above her, and he's tanned and muscular and beautiful with his teeth and eyes flashing. Then he lowers himself and kisses her shoulder and neck, and she smooths his hair (it's like petting a cat; she's reminded of the cat she had for twelve years) and looks at the ceiling, which starts out white, turns pink, and finally becomes red. When he raises himself up, he's fat and pale, and his features are horribly distorted, as if he's in terrible pain. Pamela realizes just today that he looks a lot like the Nazis in *Raiders of the Lost Ark* who get their faces melted off by the wrath of God; he looks the way the Nazis do when their faces first start melting.

TWO

The summer Pete Rose will break Ty Cobb's record for most career hits by a major-league baseball player, Lon Peterson returns home.

He's been gone six years. Now his daddy has died and left him the family farm. When he reaches Adams County in the hills of southcentral Ohio, Lon heads for the county seat, West Union, to see his daddy's lawyer. As Lon drives into town, he reads the sign saying the population is 3,658. The town is shrinking. Pete Rose has more hits than West Union has people. The front windows of Williams' Hardware, Ed's Diner, and Be Beautiful Beauty Salon are empty and cloudy with dirt; they've all shut down.

Main Street is full of potholes. Farmers are committing suicide. But Lon's daddy just died of a wrecked heart. On the phone long-distance, the lawyer said he fell over in the kitchen.

The lawyer's office is near the courthouse, next to Jack's Eats. The lawyer gets up from behind his desk, steps around it, and shakes Lon's hand. He's fragile-looking in an old gray suit. He smiles, his teeth small and yellow. Then he frowns and tells Lon he's terribly sorry about his daddy.

Lon remembers meeting him eight or nine years ago. Lon, who was fifteen or sixteen, and his daddy were coming out of the barbershop, and the lawyer was going in. They all stopped on the sidewalk, and Lon's daddy and the lawyer talked for a minute. Lon didn't listen. He saw a woman in a tight black dress walking up the steps of the courthouse across the street. Her back was to him. She had shiny blond hair and smooth slim legs. He tried to imagine her naked. Then at the top of the steps she turned around, as if she had heard someone call her name and looked down at Lon, who made a face. She was walleyed and her face flamed with acne. She quickly turned away.

The lawyer hands him some papers and says, "Have you been away from home long?"

Lon looks up from the papers. The lawyer's desk is made of dark, heavy wood, and the walls are covered with walnut paneling; there are dark bookcases and dark books. Lon feels like saying, *You mean you don't know?* Instead, he says, "You know any real-estate agents?"

When he finishes with the lawyer, Lon takes a roundabout route to the farm so that he can go past the mobile-home park. He slows down and takes a look. A collection of rusty cracker boxes on concrete blocks, swarms of dirty little kids, homely women hanging up wash. He speeds up.

The road the farm is on has never been paved, is still gravel. The neighbors and their place look unchanged. They have nine acres on the side of a rocky hill and live on their tobacco patch and county welfare. Most of the paint has peeled off their little house. Five rusty car corpses sit in the front yard. On the porch, in straight-back wooden chairs, two obese women in sleeveless dresses sit with their hands on their thighs, their tanned upper arms looking like hams. Standing by the chair of one of the fat women is a pregnant girl about eighteen. As Lon drives by, she brushes her lank hair out of her face with her hand and tucks it behind an ear and yells something at a little boy playing on the hood of one of the old cars. The child is naked except for a tee shirt with Pete Rose's face on it. Lon waves, and they all stare back.

The farm that now belongs to Lon has eighty acres. Each year, his daddy planted soy beans, alfalfa, corn, and a patch of tobacco. The house needs paint, and some of the shingles from the roof are lying in the yard, but the house looks a lot better than the tall, narrow barn, which leans way to the east and won't be standing much longer, Lon figures. When he was a kid, Lon would throw a baseball against the side of the barn and catch it on the rebound. He'd do that for hours, instead of doing his chores. He kept track of how many times he caught rebounds and how many times he missed. His daddy never painted the section of the barn where Lon's baseball wore or knocked the paint off. The barn is huge, and when it falls, there should be quite a crash.

Lon never liked life on this farm much, mainly because of the work, but looking around at all the weeds and peeling paint and rusty barbed wire, he feels sad. All this couldn't have happened in the six weeks it took the lawyer to locate him in Oregon, where he was selling encyclopedias door to door.

He realizes that this deterioration probably started the summer he left home to play minor-league baseball. The same summer his mama died of a stroke. His wife, Pamela, came home for the funeral, but no one could persuade Lon to come. He was afraid of the crying people and his mama's dead body.

Now he wishes he'd been there. The day of the funeral he played in a game in Macon, Georgia, and struck out four times.

He remembers his daddy constantly sneaking up on his mama (while she washed dishes or threw feed to the chickens—anytime) and grabbing her from behind, grabbing her big breasts and saying, "I just love milk melons."

She'd push him away and point at Lon, who would be smiling. "The boy, Frank. The boy," she'd say, her face flushed the color of a rooster's comb.

When she died, Daddy was probably broken up more than Lon ever figured. The place shows that.

Lon didn't see his daddy again after he left home to play for the Raleigh, North Carolina, Rebels. After Raleigh released him and Pamela divorced him, Lon never wrote and called only on Christmas each year from wherever he was, static filling up the gaps in the conversation.

Before he goes inside the house, Lon walks out behind the barn and looks off at the woods and thinks of growing marijuana. A lot of guys in the minors smoked it (you could afford cocaine only if you made it to the majors). When he walks back toward the house, he looks at his car, a '72 Pinto, half rust and half orange. It has bald tires and a cracked rear windshield.

He unlocks the backdoor and enters the kitchen. On the table there are stale crackers and an open jar of peanut butter and ants. In the refrigerator are three eggs, sour milk, and an empty ketchup bottle.

In the living room there are cracker crumbs on the sofa. The flowery wallpaper he remembers his mama hanging when he was still playing with toy soldiers is faded. He sees his mama sitting on his daddy's lap on the sofa. *You're a devil, Frank.*

Everything is covered with dust. The whole house smells like puke.

Let me up, Frank. There's the boy. The boy. Hi, sugar.

Six years ago, Lon stood in this living room with suitcases at his feet, his daddy hugging Pamela, his mama touching Lon's face, tears in her eyes. He was happy as hell to get out.

He turns on the old black-and-white TV. The picture is snowy but good enough. He has watched a lot of TV in the last six years and sits down on the sofa to watch a game show he's familiar with. Then he remembers the beer he bought before crossing the county line—Adams County is dry. When he goes out to the car to get it, he feels a little bit of a chill. Wispy clouds have blocked the sun, although most of the sky is bright blue. There are no sounds except the breeze in the tall grass and weeds and trees. The lawyer sold all the animals.

Lon opens all the doors and windows to air the house

out. He drinks beers in front of the TV. He drinks one can after another. When it gets dark, the sounds of crickets come through the open windows and doors. Then the sounds of things walking around in the weeds. Lon gets off the sofa and shuts the house up, then goes back to the TV and drinks more beer. He figures he'll keep drinking until he feels ready.

THREE

Lately, Pamela has been having the dream almost every night. She's scared of seeing Lon again but isn't sure why. It's been nearly six years since she saw him. Last she heard anything about him, he was in South Dakota, but that was three years ago. She's not sure she remembers what he looks like—although she knows he's neither the beautiful man nor the horrible man of her dream. She's thrown away every picture she had of him, but she has half a photograph that shows her in her high-school prom dress with a disembodied arm around her shoulders, Lon's arm.

She cries some mornings, remembering the dream, while she makes breakfast and Bobby is still asleep or in the bathroom. She has always liked having the radio on mornings because the music gets her going, but she has to turn it off now if a song from six or seven years ago comes on.

The worst thing to happen recently was seeing a movie on TV that she saw at her parents' house with Lon one New Year's Eve. Her parents weren't home, and she and Lon were watching a Marx Brothers movie because Lon thought they were really funny. Eventually, without a word and still half watching the movie, Lon started undressing her. She knew he would, but it took him longer to get around to it than she expected. While they made love on the carpet, she couldn't help glancing at the TV, the only light in the room.

She has never forgotten that Groucho was wiggling his eyebrows while Lon was on her and there was a close-up on Harpo's dopey, silent laugh at the exact moment Lon came. A public service announcement for the public library appeared as he rolled off her.

One morning last week, after *Donahue*, Pamela was changing channels, and that Marx Brothers movie was on. She sat on the floor close to the TV. After the close-up on Harpo's silent laugh, she expected a commercial, but the movie kept going. She flicked off the set and stared at her reflection in the dark screen.

Pete Rose is one reason she thinks she's having the dream more often. He is back with the Cincinnati Reds as player-manager after being gone five years, and there's a lot of hoopla about his breaking Ty Cobb's record. There's news about him every day—whether he got a hit in the most recent game.

Pete Rose was Lon's hero.

In high school, Lon was the greatest baseball player in the history of Adams County. Three days after Pamela and Lon graduated from high school, they got married. Lon wore his only suit, a dark green one, and his baseball spikes. He had polished them and wire brushed the cleats so that they shone. The minister wouldn't let him wear his baseball cap during the ceremony, but at the reception in the Methodist church's basement, Lon put it on. Bud Morris, the star pitcher of the West Union High School team, was best man and also wore spikes.

Pamela and Lon spent their wedding night at the Holiday Inn in Portsmouth. She found it strange to make love in that cool, dark room that had a smell reminding her of hospitals. People out in the hall walked past their door, laughing. She was used to his car (they made love at her parents' house only that one time) or, when his parents were gone, his room, the walls covered with pictures of famous baseball players and the top of the dresser crowded with trophies, little gold men swinging baseball bats. She loved the smell of his bed.

It was strange to make love not looking at the rip in the

convertible top of Lon's '64 Skylark or at Pete Rose's grinning gap-toothed face.

The next day they drove to Raleigh, North Carolina—almost. Lon's Skylark gave out thirty miles north of the city, and they ended up having to take a bus the rest of the way. Lon had always claimed his car was a classic and worth a pile of money, but he paid forty dollars to have it towed to a junk yard. Pamela found it hard to believe he could be so wrong about something.

There was a used-car dealer in Raleigh who sponsored a late-night movie, and as the summer wore on, Pamela paid closer and closer attention to the cars the dealer showed off. She sat on the threadbare sofa in her and Lon's furnished apartment near the ball park and watched movies like *Zombie Brides* hosted by this car-hawking man in a vampire costume. Between segments of the movie, The Vampire stood in a well-lighted car lot in front of used cars, his pale face and blood-red lips always smiling, telling stupid jokes, reading fan mail, and talking about cars: "We have late-night specials on all our quality pre-owned cars. We're open all night. Our salesmen are ready to serve you. Come on down between midnight and four, and you can be on TV." Sometimes while talking about a car, he would lay hands on it, his palms flat on the hood, as if blessing it or driving out all the gremlins. Every once in a while, he held somebody's elbow and said, "Tell us your name."

"Edward Dixon."

"Ed just bought that '71 Monte Carlo I showed you earlier," The Vampire said to the camera. "He beat the rest of you folks to it, but come on down anyway. We have plenty of cars. Ed, you want to say hi to anybody?"

"My wife."

"Okay."

"Hi, Irene." He gave a little wave, his shoulders slightly hunched. He reminded Pamela of Gomer Pyle. A lot of people in North Carolina did.

"Okay. Thank you, Edward Dixon." Pointing at the camera, The Vampire said, "You, too, can be on TV. Just come on down and take a look at our cars."

One night, near the end of the summer and the baseball season, alone because Lon was on a road trip, Pamela felt a strong urge to go down to The Vampire's lot and buy a '71 Camaro he kept showing off. She still thinks about that Camaro every once in a while, and when she does, she feels she missed an opportunity, missed taking a road that would have led to another life entirely. California comes to her mind. A hot sun. But a cool breeze, too.

It was only $750. She thought about the money in her and Lon's bank account, around $800, most of which her parents had given them. She had always liked Camaros, although she liked Trans Ams best. When the Skylark broke down, Lon told her that after he made it to the major leagues he'd buy her a brand new, fully loaded Trans Am.

By July, though, she knew she'd never get it.

FOUR

Lon never feels quite ready and passes out sometime during a rerun of *Love Boat*. When he wakes up, Wile E. Coyote is falling off a cliff, and The Roadrunner is saying "beep beep."

He rubs his eyes and staggers to the kitchen where rusty water comes out of the faucet. When it clears up, he puts his mouth to the faucet and drinks a long time. Then he slides the plastic checkered curtains apart and looks at a field that's a mess of grass and weeds.

He remembers he dreamed about Pamela, although he can't recall the details of the dream. It was she he was trying to get ready for last night. Distance has always helped him not to think about her much, but since he started the drive across the country from Oregon, she's been on his mind a lot. Now that she is so close, he feels he has to see her. He hasn't the slightest idea what will happen when he sees her or what he'll feel, but he can't help thinking that she's the only woman who can give him something he needs—some complex yet essential thing he can't put a label on.

A lot of Vietnam vets, Lon has heard, have flashbacks and nightmares, and that's supposed to be why they can't live normal lives. Lon told a counselor at the junior college he attended one semester in California that he knew how those vets felt. They'd failed; he'd failed. The counselor smiled. Lon had gone to him because he never felt like studying. All he wanted to do was watch TV and sleep and get laid. The counselor said that baseball and Vietnam weren't at all alike. One was war, the other a game. Just a game. It wasn't really a very significant thing, a person would realize if he thought about it. The world could get along fine—in fact, a lot of people in the world did get along fine without baseball, he said, still smiling, his fingers twined together on top of his big desk.

When Lon was in elementary school, he read biographies of the baseball greats—Babe Ruth, Lou Gehrig. The books said they were great men, beloved national heroes. He also read biographies of Abraham Lincoln and George Washington, and there was no difference between the presidents and the baseball players—the books all sounded the same.

In the seventies, when the Cincinnati Reds won six divisional titles, they were front-page news in Cincinnati: REDS WIN EIGHTH IN ROW. At the bottom of the page, below a picture of Pete Rose or Joe Morgan or Johnny Bench, below the picture's caption or pushed to page two, would be a headline like EARTHQUAKE KILLS THOUSANDS IN SOUTH AMERICA.

Lon looked at the counselor, matched his smile, and said the world could get along without war, too, couldn't it?

While looking out the window over the kitchen sink, Lon notices his Pinto has a flat tire.

He looks in the cabinets for breakfast foods, but all he finds is a bag of white beans and an unopened bottle of ketchup. His daddy loved white beans smothered in ketchup. Lon suddenly sees his daddy's heart pumping blood. Opening and closing like a fist. Then the image gets crazy, and the heart looks old, sprouts gray hairs and warts. Lon goes into the living room and turns off the TV. In the silence, he shivers.

He puts the spare tire on and kicks it. Then he kicks the Pinto's fender. He kicks the passenger door. The car rocks. He kicks the front bumper.

He backs away, his heart pounding, then turns toward the woods. "Marijuana," he says out loud. He walks toward the woods. Under the trees it's cool and dark. He decides he won't grow marijuana. He thinks of jail. He's been there and didn't like it. He woke up in a small cell in Texas with dried blood and puke all down his shirt, one of the sleeves torn off. And when he remembers this, he remembers a nightclub that used to be a chicken house, a hundred-and-fifty-foot cinder-block building with antique chicken-plucking machines in the corners and a nude dancer named Reba, who had a shaved pussy.

No, he's not going to grow marijuana, but he's also not going to be a goddamned farmer.

In the afternoon, in the middle of The Game-of-the-Week (St. Louis is playing Chicago), the real-estate agent Lon has been expecting drives up the long gravel driveway in a big Buick. The agent has bushy eyebrows and an olive complexion; his skin looks greasy. He has a white shirt on with the sleeves rolled up, and a bright green tie. His fingers are thick and short, and he grips Lon's hand a little too firmly.

While Lon shows him around, the agent keeps saying, "Okay. Okay."

"My daddy let the place get run down."

"Well, he was old."

"He was sixty-one."

"You know, Lon, what would really make the value of this property shoot up?"

"I'm plannin' to do some work around the place."

"Besides that."

"What?"

"If somebody killed your neighbors and burned their house." He makes a squawking noise.

Lon turns away so the guy can't see he's not even smiling and looks in the direction of the neighbors' place. They always had a swarm of kids, and he never knew all their names. The neighbors tended not to have anything to do with anybody outside their family. But Lon remembers three grubby little kids, two boys and a girl, coming across the soy-bean field one day and up to the house to ask him for his autograph. No one had ever asked for his autograph before. Hell, he was only in high school. He went into his room and got three sheets of notebook paper and signed each one, making the letters of his name short and fat the way Pete Rose did.

The agent clears his throat and says it's a good idea to fix the place up. It can bring thirty-five thousand if they find some city people looking for a rural retreat and a tax break. Those kinds of buyers have been keeping the real-estate business going all right in this area, he says.

As he's about to leave, opening the door of his Buick, releasing new-car smell, the agent says, "By the way, I remember when you played ball at the high school."

Lon shrugs and grins, nods.

"You were the best damn player anybody'd ever seen around here. I remember that."

Lon looks up at the sun, squints, and says, "Thank you."

He drives recklessly on his way to Brown County to get beer. He feels good. A hundred feet past the county line, he stops at the Hilltop Store, a little place run by a bent, slow old woman, who has been selling beer to minors since World War II. Lon remembers skidding on the gravel lot up to the front door of the Hilltop in his Skylark, six or seven buddies—sometimes the whole starting lineup of the West

Union High School baseball team—squeezed in the front and back seats. When he was sixteen, Lon would strut into the Hilltop, pick up a six-pack, and all the old woman ever said was, "Anything else, honey?"

He has never known her name. And now she looks the same, the old loose long dress with a small flower print, bald spots showing through the wisps of her white hair.

"How you doin' today, ma'am?" Lon says, setting three six-packs on the counter.

"Anything else, honey?"

"Nope."

She makes change from an old cigar box. Lon looks around, smells something he associates with old people's houses, but he doesn't know what it is. All the canned foods are covered with thin layers of dust. There's rust on some of the cans. Lon wonders what the expiration dates on them are. He thinks about how easy it would be to rob this woman.

Then without thinking about it, he says, "It's been a long time since I been in Ohio."

She counts out his change.

"But I grew up round here. Ma'am?" He's not sure she's listening. She's looking into her cigar box. "Ma'am? Do you remember me?"

She puts the cigar box under the counter and turns aside, her left hand on her hip, her chin on her chest as if she's looking at her feet. "Yes," she says.

"You do?"

"Yes."

Before he pulls out onto the road, he opens a can. He's ecstatic. With thirty-five thousand dollars he can buy a new car and some nice clothes, and he's got an idea—a good idea for a change. He's going to become a real-estate agent in Adams and Brown counties. A lot of local people will remember him from his high school playing days, and the city people from Cincinnati looking for rural retreats will take to him fast because everybody from Cincinnati is a baseball nut. In any case, people will definitely like him better than that dork trying to sell his daddy's farm.

Like the Reds, Lon was once front-page news—at least in Adams County in the *West Union Gazette* and *The Adams County Courier.* He hit .436 his senior year, was county Most Valuable Player three years. Scouts from New York, Chicago, Cincinnati, Cleveland, and Pittsburgh came to Adams County to see him play, sat in the rickety old bleachers and wrote in little notebooks and shook his hand and put their arms around his manager's shoulders and ducked their heads, asking questions about him in low voices (*We need to know everything you can tell us*), and Mr. Daniels nodded emphatically and shook his head vigorously, wanting to see one of his players make it to the big time.

Jesus, Lon thinks, if he could go back and freeze his life at that time, just be in high school for eternity. . . . For Christ's sake, he screwed three of the school's five cheerleaders.

He drives around, drinking, looking at houses and farm land. He could have a real-estate office in West Union. It amazes him now that for all those years he was afraid to come home. What was he afraid of?

He feels higher than he's felt for a long time, and he heads out to the mobile-home park. He's ready.

FIVE

Pamela has to park in a far corner of the McDonald's lot because Ray, the manager, won't let any of his girls park near the store. She thinks it's strange that Ray calls the place a store instead of a restaurant. And she's a little put off by the way he calls her and her co-workers "his girls." When she shuts off the engine, the Maverick shudders. The smells of Big Macs and french fries and exhaust fumes are in the air.

It's four in the afternoon, and they're getting ready for the supper-time rush. Pamela works mornings sometimes, evenings other times—whenever she's needed; sometimes she works double shifts.

Working the register is not too bad; it's a lot better than clearing off the tables of customers who don't bother to put their trash in garbage cans. Half-eaten Quarter Pounders with ketchup and mustard oozing out make her a little sick. Occasionally, somebody will chew up part of a hamburger, then spit it out on the tray. She wonders whether people sometimes do that out of meanness, the way Betty Jo Jenkins spits on the hamburgers and french fries when Ray's not around and says, "Just a little seasoning. We do it all for you." Betty Jo is a big fat trashy woman who recently lost her welfare because she had a man living with her and her five kids.

Mary Engler, a seventeen-year-old who attends The Church of Christ, is horrified by Betty Jo, but Carla, who brags all the time that she's going to get married instead of finishing high school, seems to just think Betty Jo's a greaseball.

"My fiancé showed me a cartoon in a dirty magazine?" Carla says. Ray has just left after giving Pamela her instructions for today. He frequently disappears for forty minutes or an hour. Carla and Betty Jo say they'd bet he's got a woman. "Well, in this cartoon it shows this girl in a McDonald's uniform crouched under a table doin' you-know-what with her mouth to some guy that's eating a Big Mac and smilin' real big." Carla demonstrates the smile. "Underneath the picture it said, 'We do it *all* for you.' Ain't that the funniest thing you ever heard?"

Betty Jo says, "Why don't you ask Ray if you can start doin' that?"

"Sometimes you're really disgusting, you know that?" Carla says.

"Nobody likes a tease, honey."

Pamela acts as if she's not paying attention. She doesn't have much to do with her co-workers. Except for Betty Jo and Ray, they're all in high school. None of them has a nickel's worth of knowledge about life.

Pamela laughs to herself when the girls fantasize out loud about getting married, but she never says anything. What's the point? She knows what it's like to be sixteen, seventeen, and to think all you need is a certain boy, roof over your head, a TV, and a bed—paradise.

Mary Engler says she's proud to be a virgin and plans to stay that way until her wedding night.

Carla says, "Well, I'm willin' to do anything for Rick. We're gettin' married anyway."

"That doesn't make it right. What if he broke up with you? What if he got killed or something?"

"You ever have the opportunity to lose it, Mary?" Betty Jo says.

"I'll do anything to keep Rick. I'd kill myself if he ever broke up with me."

"That's a sin, too."

"I love him."

"You should love Jesus more than anybody else."

Pamela suddenly remembers what Bobby looked like when he was a kid, skinny and pale, his hair long and lank. He grew up across the street from her, but she and Bobby never played together. Bobby never played with anybody. He was weird and little girls didn't want to sit next to him or stand next in line to him, including Pamela. When he was fourteen and fifteen years old, he still went trick or treating, walking the streets alone with a feed sack designed to hold a hundred pounds of shelled horse corn. He'd dress up like Snoopy or Adolph Hitler or Jesus Christ.

But he seemed sweet—and merely different—when Pamela came back home from North Carolina. At first, after the divorce, she dated Lon's friends, boys like Lon, jocks. When they'd come to her parents' house to pick her up, Bobby was often on his porch across the street. He sat on his porch year-round; in freezing weather he'd be sitting in the porch swing, smoking a cigarette. In summer, he'd sit there without a shirt. His chest was pale and smooth, and

Pamela always thought of a porcelain doll. When she went out on her dates, after the divorce, she'd give Bobby a little wave, mainly just because he was a neighbor. He'd nod and give her a shy smile.

On the dates, the boys talked about themselves. Sometimes they asked about Lon, how he was doing, what he was doing. They asked her why Lon had such a bad year.

Then they grabbed her crotch and said, "Come on. You've been married."

Bobby took her to the Smoky Mountains for their honeymoon, a *real* honeymoon. Pamela considered it a good start. Each day of the trip, Bobby gave her a gift first thing in the morning: a stuffed Smokey the Bear, a silver-plated necklace, a pair of hoop earrings, a bottle of Love's Baby Soft perfume, a music box that played "My Darling Clementine." He snuck off to buy the presents at gift shops near the motel while she napped or sunbathed or watched TV.

The sixth morning, Bobby went through his usual routine: he sat on the edge of their bed, touched her shoulder, and said, "Wake up, baby. I got you a surprise."

Pamela sat up, cradling her Smokey the Bear, smiling. The slim straps on her nightgown had slipped off her shoulders. It took her eyes a moment to focus on the present Bobby held just a few inches from her face: a varnished outhouse about ten inches high with "john" sloppily painted across the door. "What is it?"

"Open the door." Bobby moved the outhouse even closer to her face.

When she opened the little door, thinking that maybe the real gift was inside, a grinning toothless plastic hillbilly with a disproportionately large penis squirted a thin stream of water on her face.

Bobby fell off the bed and rolled on the floor like some fool on TV, maybe even a cartoon character, Pamela thought.

"That's disgusting." She wiped at her cheek and sniffed her hand. "That's just water I hope."

"Hell no!"

"Ugh!"

"Yeah, it's only water." Bobby got up off the floor.

"It's still disgusting."

"I think it's funny as hell."

She and Bobby had drunk a lot of wine the night before, and now she was aware of her headache.

"It's stupid. That's what it is."

Bobby's face scrunched up so fast Pamela thought for a second she was dreaming. He glared and turned the color of raw steak. "Listen, woman, one of these days I might just be *gone*."

SIX

The trailers are beat up and old. Lon drives slow, looking at the names on mailboxes. He vaguely remembers the guy Pamela's married to. The guy didn't play any sports. When Lon finds Pamela's mobile home, he stays in his car, looking at it while he finishes a beer. The trailer is a two-tone aqua and white sixties model with an air conditioner sticking out a front window, chugging and dripping. He remembers a picture Pamela drew one time of the big house they were going to build after he made it to the major leagues and was making a million dollars a year.

It was going to be a brick house, she explained, because brick houses were safer in bad storms. The master bedroom would be huge with a round bed in the center of it. There would be a bedroom for each child, one boy and two girls, and the living room would have a big picture window; he and Pamela would look out at green mountains. The living room was to be painted gold.

SEVEN

She comes home and the screen door has a hole in it. It's hot outside, but the trailer is icy because Bobby has apparently let the window air conditioner run nonstop all day again. Pamela thinks of the electric bill.

Bobby's sitting in the dark.

"Don't turn on the light," he says.

"Why not?"

"Just don't."

"I have to see, don't I?"

"Don't."

She flicks the switch. Bobby's tee shirt is torn. He's holding his gun in his lap. It's a little .22 pistol he bought not long ago.

"What's goin' on?" she says, scared.

"Nothin'."

A stack of *True Crime* magazines sits on the coffee table, which is chipped at every corner, the particle board showing. Bobby started reading *True Crime* after he lost his job.

Pamela remembers that in high school a girl named Linda Sharp read *True Crime* in the lunch room. One day Linda told her about a woman who came out of her shower and found a man with a gun in her bedroom. He made her lie down on her bed naked, and he put the gun inside her and got her all worked up. Then he pulled the trigger.

Linda was smiling and her eyes looked weird. The woman lived, she added after a minute. At the time, Pamela thought Linda was just gross. Now she feels really sorry for her.

Pamela feels Bobby's eyes on her as she walks into the kitchenette and puts her purse on the counter.

"Lon was here," he says.

She feels light, as if she could float, but for a minute she can't even move her feet.

EIGHT

It's morning, and Bobby is in the woods behind the mobile-home park, shooting holes in an old cake pan he leaned against an oak tree. He bought the gun a few weeks ago after he donated a couple of his antique toys to the Brown County Hospital children's ward. He thought he deserved to give himself a present, so he bought the .22

pistol. He pretends the cake pan is the face of Pamela's ex-husband.

When he goes back to the trailer, Pamela is wearing her McDonald's uniform and washing the breakfast dishes. Bobby stands on the other side of the counter that separates the kitchen and the living room. He puts the pistol on the counter and looks at the pancake syrup on the plates Pamela's washing and remembers how bad the pancakes were; Pamela bought generic pancake mix again.

"Can't you steal us some Egg McMuffins?" he says. "I like Egg McMuffins and them sausage biscuits. Don't you get no fringe benefits, like all the Egg McMuffins your husband can eat?"

Pamela looks sideways at the gun and says, "You know I don't like that thing laying around."

"It ain't like we got kids that would get hold of it."

"Yeah, well, I just don't like it. I'm always afraid it's gonna get knocked on the floor and go off or something."

"There ain't nothin' to be afraid of." Bobby snatches up the pistol, puts the barrel to his temple, and pulls the trigger. Click.

Pamela staggers back from the sink with both hands on her heart. "One of these days you're gonna kill yourself."

When she takes them away from her chest, her wet hands leave a print on her blouse. Bobby aims at the print and pulls the trigger.

"What the hell's the matter with you?" Pamela yells.

"It ain't loaded, stupid."

"You're gonna shoot yourself or somebody else if you don't stop playing around."

"I guarantee you I'll shoot Lon if he ever comes around here again."

Pamela stares at the dirty dish water and pulls the stopper out of the sink, but the water just stands there. "Stopped up *again*," she mumbles.

"You hear me, woman?"

"If I bring you home a Big Mac, will you promise to settle

down?"

"I'd rather have Taco Bell. Why don't you get a job at Taco Bell?"

Pamela walks fast to their bedroom. "I got to get going."

Bobby follows her. She's slim, and he's always liked the way she walks. In their bedroom, she looks through her purse. "I've got to get going," she says again.

"I do, too," Bobby says, grabbing her and pulling her down onto the bed. He gets on top of her.

"I have to go to work," Pamela says, as though she's worn out.

Bobby pins her wrists on either side of her head, not to hurt her, just to keep her from getting up. He's wearing a sleeveless tee shirt and notices how skinny his arms are. He's been meaning to buy a set of weights and start working out.

"Let me up."

She closes her eyes, and he notices for the first time this morning how pretty her face is. When they were in high school, she was a cheerleader, and he knew she thought he was shit. He kisses her.

"Okay, can I get up now? I'm gonna be late. I might really have to go to work at Taco Bell if you don't let me up."

"I'm sorry I scared you in the kitchen."

"I hear they put dog food in their tacos."

He kisses her again and lets go of her wrists so that he can fondle her, and she pushes him away and gets off the bed. She looks in the dresser mirror and straightens her uniform and pats her hair back into place.

"One time when I was in Cincinnati," Bobby says, lying on the bed, watching her, "I saw a guy in a porno movie that kept talkin' about hittin' home runs and had a thing about as long as a goddamn baseball bat. I thought about that guy yesterday when Lon come here, sniffin' around like all these years hadn't went by and you wasn't married to me, askin' to see you."

"I'll see you tonight. If I don't work a double shift, you

want me to bring you a Big Mac for your supper or not?"

"Pam, I wanta ask you one thing before you go."

"Well, hurry up."

"Did Lon have a thing as big as a baseball bat?"

Pamela walks out of the bedroom. Bobby hears the front door open and slam, then the Maverick grinding and grinding and grinding, until it finally catches.

With *The Price Is Right* on, Bobby sits on the sofa with newspaper spread on the coffee table and cleans his gun. When he's done, he goes into the bathroom, brushes his teeth, shaves, and smears deodorant under his arms. He does body-builder poses in front of the mirror. He doesn't look all that bad, he thinks. He sure as hell would rather be skinny than fat. Big guys die young. Then he puts on a clean tee shirt, and he's ready to go see Becky Diane.

Bobby has gotten to like the freedom of his days. He doesn't look at want ads much anymore. He used to fill out job applications for factory jobs and construction work all over southcentral Ohio and even in Kentucky a couple of times, although he considers Kentucky a hillbilly dumping ground and the worst state in America, except maybe for West Virginia. He applied for a lot more jobs than he told Pamela he did. He didn't want her to know how many people were turning him down. It was better to have her think he was lazy.

When he filled out an application at the office of a man who owned a construction company, Bobby got the idea of becoming an antique-toy dealer. In the waiting room old toys sat in display cases. When Bobby asked the secretary about them, she pointed to a rusty little truck and said, "The boss paid two hundred dollars for that thing. I wouldn't give you a nickel. But he loves those things. He dusts them off himself. Won't even let me touch them."

"Two hundred dollars?"

"That old beat-up thing over there, that tricycle—that cost him three hundred and fifty."

"Jesus H. Christ."

Driving into West Union, Bobby has his gun under the front seat. Every couple of minutes he reaches down and touches it.

He pulls his '69 Dodge Dart into a parking space in front of the courthouse. Becky Diane works in the drivers license bureau.

A farmer in overalls, who looks about eighty, is trying to read the eye chart. Bobby stands in the doorway. The farmer can't get any of the letters right, and Becky Diane says, "No, Harold. Let's try one more time." She always asks people to read the third row of letters. Bobby wonders why the people in line who can't see don't just listen to the people in front of them and memorize the line: A Z B D E L.

The farmer guesses wrong again. "I'm sorry, Harold," Becky Diane says, "but I can't renew your license." She talks loud and slow, and the old man is bent toward her, frozen. "But there's an eye doctor in Peebles that'll sign a paper for you, and you bring it here, and I'll give you your new license."

Becky Diane smiles when she sees Bobby. She's thirty-five, ten years older than Bobby, but she still lives with her mother. Becky Diane is wall-eyed and has bad acne scars. She's thin except for a little bit of a potbelly. The first time Bobby took her to the Route 33 Motel, three months ago, she couldn't stop shivering, and she bled on the sheets. Bobby licked her belly and said, "You sure you don't have a tumor or somethin'?"

Last week she announced to Bobby that she'd been doing sit-ups and said, "Doesn't my stomach look a lot flatter?"

Today, during her lunch hour, they go to a hollow outside of town and park. He shows her how good he's become with his pistol, shooting holes in the trunk of a skinny maple tree. Then he lets her shoot. She flinches each time she fires and can't hit the big tree she's aiming at. "This is really hard," she says. "You're really good."

He unbuttons her blouse and cups his hands over her small pointed breasts. "You ain't like other women. If I wasn't married already, I'd marry you."

She strokes his face, and he kisses her fingers. Her hands are beautiful. Her fingernails are long and a different color every day. She gets manicures whenever she has her hair done, once a week. Her hair is thick and blond. Bobby has always heard men and boys say Becky Diane is a good-looking woman from the back. Last week at the motel, he told her to turn over and get on her knees. He pretended he was with Stevie Nicks.

"I love you, baby," he says and takes her hand and leads her to the car. He opens the back door, and she lies down with her skirt hiked up. He pulls her panties down over her shoes and buries his face in her neck. She makes little sounds that remind him of mice. When he's done, she wants to kiss, but he pulls back.

"I don't feel like it. Jesus, you're ugly." And he thinks about how pretty Pamela is.

"Why do you do this?" Becky Diane says, straightening her clothes. Bobby ignores her. "You do this all the time. Half the time we make love. It's sweet and nice, and then you ruin it like this."

Bobby picks up his gun off the hood of the car and aims at a tree. He hears her sniffling. He pulls the trigger. Click. Then again. Click. Then again. Click. He puts the barrel to his temple. Click.

When he stops in front of the courthouse to let her out, she's still crying a little. Her face is covered with pink splotches. After she gets out, she bends down to the window and says, "How about tonight? Can you get away? I'll tell Mother I'm going to the library or something."

"I might not be able to see you ever again," Bobby says.

"Why not, Bobby? Why not?"

"Cause I have decided to shoot somebody this afternoon. That's why."

He drives toward Peebles, where the McDonald's is. West Union is a dead town with shut-down stores, pot holes, and a bunch of old loafers sitting around whittling. Peebles, though, always seems busy—a lot of cars and trucks, and besides the McDonald's, there are Taco Bell and Pizza Hut and the Big Boy drive-in restaurant.

On his way to Peebles, he thinks about yesterday when Lon showed up. Lon was drunk and unshaven. He was driving a beat-up Pinto. Yeah, the big baseball star looked bad.

Bobby had been napping on the sofa. The trailer was cold from the window air conditioner running all day, and all the lights were off. Bobby liked lying in the dark, chilly trailer and drifting off to sleep, then waking up to find the afternoon and half the evening gone and Pamela due home soon.

Lon banged on the screen door and woke him up.

Bobby looked at him through the screen door and smelled beer.

"How you been, Bobby?"

"I ain't had no work in a year. But Pam's workin' at the McDonald's over at Peebles."

"I figured Pamela would be home since it's Sunday. My daddy died, you know. Left me his farm. I just wanted to say hi to her."

"She's workin' right now."

Lon nodded. "You know this is the first time I been back to Ohio in six years. I been everywhere."

"You been to Hawaii?"

"No, but I been to most of the states out west."

Bobby nodded.

"My real-estate agent says I might get nearly forty thousand for the place. Daddy didn't owe on it. I'm thinking of getting into real estate myself."

Bobby stared straight at him, but Lon was looking up at the sky. He kept looking up there. Then he shoved his arm through the flimsy screen and grabbed Bobby's tee shirt and said, "I can tell you exactly how she sounds when she's about to come."

Bobby got away and backed into the darkness of the trailer. "Don't you come in this house." He was shaking and bumped into the sofa. He sat down.

"House?" Lon said. "Shit."

"She told me you was crazy. She told me how you used to bust up your apartment after you messed up in games, makin' her think you was gonna kill her, and then tellin' your old man you was doin' great when he phoned you."

"I never once hit Pamela," Lon said and hit the frame of the screen door with the heel of his hand.

"Said you threw things and punched walls."

"I never hit her, God knows."

"It was in the paper here about you battin' one-fifty. Everybody was talkin' about what a big disappointment you was. And nobody was real surprised when Pam come back home."

Bobby saw Lon reach for the door handle. He could have come in, but didn't. His hand dropped to his side, and he said, "Bobby?"

"What?"

"Pamela has a big mole right next to her pussy."

"I know all about it."

"You goddamn hick. You never done anything or been anybody."

For a minute the only sound was the chugging of the air conditioner. It seemed awfully loud.

Then Bobby said, "Lon?"

"What?"

"She's growed a new mole."

"What?"

"She's growed a new mole. Right on the other side of her pussy."

As soon as Bobby heard the door of Lon's Pinto slam, he thought of his pistol in the nightstand in the bedroom.

NINE

Lon wakes up in his old room. Posters of baseball super-stars are still on all four walls after all these years, yellow-ing and curling up at the edges. He opens the closet door and touches the sleeve of his high-school uniform. He thinks about buying lightweight, colorful clothes and go-ing to Miami to live and maybe become a vice cop. He likes "Miami Vice."

He drinks a New Coke for breakfast and looks at part of some new soap opera. Pamela comes to mind, and he says out loud, "Screw her."

After shutting off the TV, he starts reading volume six of the *New World Encyclopedia*. It's the only volume he still has, a salesman's sample. He got into the habit of reading volumes of the encyclopedia when he was selling them in Oregon. Sometimes, when he didn't feel like bothering people, he would find a park or a playground or a shop-ping center and sit down on a bench and read his samples. He started by looking up famous baseball players. Pete Rose was in there. Then he started reading articles at ran-dom. He doesn't care what the subject is. He opens the book to any page. He wonders why he couldn't study when he was going to that junior college.

He decides to drive into Peebles for lunch. When he passes the McDonald's, he sees a crowd of people inside. He goes down a couple of more blocks, then pulls into the Big Boy Restaurant, where he can get curb service.

When the girl brings his order, she hangs the tray on his window and pauses after he pays her. "Do I know you?" she says.

Lon squints at her. She's wearing a stupid-looking cap with a little fat boy holding a burger on it. She has fiery orange hair, a pale complexion and bright red lipstick. Her tee shirt has the same little fat boy on it the cap does.

"Do you?" Lon says.

"You just look familiar."

She's slim and her jeans are tight. She steps back, maybe so that Lon can see her better, and cocks her hips and puts her hand on her side.

Sixteen, Lon thinks. "You might know me."

"No. I think I was wrong."

"I'm famous."

She looks at the Pinto.

"I didn't say I was rich."

"Yeah, well, I gotta go," she says. She looks at him for a moment longer before she turns and walks back to the restaurant.

While he eats his burger, Lon watches her carrying trays to other cars. When she comes to take his tray away, he says, "Do I know you?"

"Sure. I'm famous," she says.

"I bet you're rich, too."

"I'm the richest kid at West Union High School."

"You a freshman?"

"Senior in the fall. I can't wait to get out."

"I went there. Graduated a long time ago, though."

"You know that girl that became a movie star?"

"Yvonne Strickland? Those stupid horror movies?"

"Yeah, that's her name."

"She was long before my time. I graduated in seventy-nine."

"You oughta be able to apply for social security soon."

Lon grins. "I'm Lon Peterson."

"You a famous actor?"

"I was on the baseball team."

"I know," she says matter-of-factly.

"You know?"

"Sure. There's a picture of you in the trophy case in the lobby at school."

She turns and starts toward the restaurant. Then she stops and turns back. "But in that picture you look a lot different."

TEN

Lunch time is over. It's the quiet part of the afternoon at the McDonald's. Pamela isn't behind the counter, just a fat woman. "Hey, Betty Jo," Bobby says. He finds Pamela in the grill area, pouring a bag of frozen fries into a wire basket.

"You're not allowed back here," she says.

"I don't see what trouble I'm makin'."

"Ray said he didn't want you coming around here to see me when I'm working."

"Can I have some of them McDonaldland cookies?"

"If you pay for them." Pamela lowers the basket full of fries into hot oil and the fries hiss.

"Lon hasn't been here to see you, has he?"

"No. Is that what you came here to find out?"

"Damn, you're snappy. You know, sometimes I don't think you love me no more."

Ray walks in. "Bobby, what are you doing here?"

"I came to see my wife about a very important matter."

"Well, your wife is my employee."

"What does that mean?"

Pamela says, "It means, Bobby, that you're interfering with my work."

"I was gonna buy my lunch here."

"You don't buy it back here," Ray says.

"Okay, I'll leave."

"Thank you," Pamela says.

"But, Pam, I want you to always remember I love you, no matter what happens this afternoon."

Ray shakes his head. His face is red.

On his way out, Bobby stops at the condiment center and stuffs his pockets full of straws and packets of ketchup and salt.

In his car, he reaches under the seat and touches his gun. He should blow Ray away. He thinks of an antique dealer in Cincinnati—"Boy, most of this stuff you've been buying is junk. You've got to learn what's rare and what's not.

You've got to try to buy things that are in good condition. Have you looked at any of the price guides?" Bobby should blow him away, too.

The house Lon's daddy left him sits far back off the gravel road. The long driveway is full of ruts. Bobby doesn't see Lon's Pinto anywhere.

The farm is quiet. The wind rustles the high grass around the house, which has lost most of its paint and gone a shade of gray that makes Bobby think of cancer.

The back door is unlocked, and Bobby enters the kitchen with his pistol raised. The house smells like puke. In the living room, beer cans are scattered in front of the TV.

In the hall, he catches sight of himself in a mirror mounted on the wall: a skinny man in a tee shirt, his pants pockets bulging with straws and packets of ketchup and salt, a black gun in his hand; his hair is stuck to his forehead, and sweat slides down his red face.

He steps into Lon's bedroom. On the walls are yellowing pictures of baseball players. On the night table and the dresser and on a table in a corner are tarnished trophies.

Bobby opens the closet. Baseball uniforms hang there. Under them are stacked newspapers—the *West Union Gazette* and the *Adams County Courier*—with Lon's name in the headlines. Bobby lifts them, uncovering a stack of *Playboy* magazines.

Bobby remembers the way Lon was in high school. Stuck on himself. Lon never talked to him. Bobby heard he screwed every cheerleader in the school.

After laying the gun on top of them, he picks up the stack of *Playboys*. In the hall, he sees himself in the mirror again—still sweating, even redder in the face, his arms full of pictures of naked women.

ELEVEN

"You want to have something to drink?" Lon asks, opening the refrigerator and seeing only two cans of beer.

Cindy has walked on into the living room, checking the place out, and Lon feels embarrassed about the looks of the place. "No, thanks."

"Just as well."

"Your maid got the decade off?"

Lon goes into the living room. Cindy is looking at a painting of a clown on the wall. Lon did it from a paint-by-number set when he was nine years old. She's taken the stupid cap off, but she's still wearing the tee shirt.

Lon's palms are sweaty, and he keeps wiping them on his jeans. "You want to be my maid?"

"No way."

"I'm gonna be rich after I sell this place."

"So where are all these trophies you wanted to show me?"

"They're in here. This is my bedroom." She follows him in. "I grew up in this room."

She looks around. "Your trophies are tarnished. You should take better care of them."

"I haven't looked at them for six years."

"I have twelve ribbons from gymnastics meets."

For what seems like a long time, neither one of them talks. The sun is setting, and the room is getting dark. Lon steps closer to her, and she doesn't move. "Hey, come here."

"I was just curious," she says, turning toward him.

He puts his hands on her waist and kisses her. Then she steps back and says, "Let's go some place."

Lon has a feeling she's a tease. "We just got here."

"Don't let your blood pressure get too high, old man. You don't want to have a stroke."

"So where you wanta go?"

"Starlite Drive-in. It'll be dark soon. You wanta take me?"

"What's showin'?"

"One of those *Friday the Thirteenth* movies."

"Okay. Why not? I'm a man of leisure."

When they drive past the McDonald's, he looks over. The place is almost empty and all lit up inside. The front has big windows, and he sees Pamela standing behind the counter.

"What's wrong?" Cindy says.

"Nothin'."

At the drive-in, Cindy keeps calling kids over to the car and saying, "Hey, what's happenin'?" and then introducing them to Lon. Lon feels old. He nods toward the kids and then ignores them, playing with his car keys. The boys Cindy calls over are all lanky and retarded looking with peach-fuzz mustaches and goatees.

After the movie starts, whenever some dumb teenager is about to get his head split open or his guts ripped out (Lon thinks it's almost funny it's so stupid), Cindy clutches his arm and digs in her fingernails.

He tries not to think about her, but Pamela keeps coming to mind. In the movie, a cat gets chopped in half, and Lon thinks about the cat Pamela used to have. Puff was about fourteen years old when Pamela took him to Raleigh. Lon never paid any attention to the cat. Then it died the third or fourth week in North Carolina. Pamela claimed the move was too much for the poor thing. Damn cat. She cried for days—and there Lon was, having the worst time of his life—and shipped the corpse back to Ohio by UPS so that her mother could bury Puff in the back yard.

Lon stops watching the movie. He looks at Cindy out of the corner of his eye. Her mouth is open a little and her eyes are wide, as if she's really into the movie. The next time she digs her fingernails into his arm, he grabs her and kisses her on the mouth. Then he kisses her neck and holds her and won't let her loose.

TWELVE

Bobby calls Becky Diane and tells her to come to his trailer tonight. Pamela is working a double shift.

Bobby and Becky Diane sit on the sofa, watching a TV

show about near-death experiences. People talk about floating above their bodies, watching doctors and nurses give them shots, hang drug drips, and pound on their hearts. They talk about rising a thousand miles a second, leaving the planet, and being surrounded by warm, comforting lights, about seeing dead relatives or Jesus.

When the show goes off, Becky Diane says, "Why do you think some people are met by relatives and others by Jesus and then other people see old friends or like that one man who saw his second-grade teacher?"

"Maybe you get met by whoever you want to meet you."

"What if you've been married about eight times like Elizabeth Taylor?"

"I want to be met by Marilyn Monroe."

"My Aunt Sylvia would want to be greeted at the gates of heaven by nobody other than Elvis."

"Yeah, I bet Elvis keeps pretty busy."

Bobby turns off the TV. When he sits back down, he sees himself in the blank screen, a tiny man far away.

"I knew you didn't mean it this afternoon," Becky Diane says.

"Mean what?"

"What you said about shooting somebody."

Bobby doesn't say anything for a minute. Then he says, "I decided to spare his life. But I could of shot him. He trespassed on my property and assaulted me."

"Who?"

"Nobody."

They both stare at the blank TV.

"Don't you want to do something?" Becky Diane says, putting her hand on his thigh.

"I grew up right across the street from her."

"Who?"

"My wife."

"Oh." Becky Diane takes her hand off Bobby's leg.

"I used to watch her goin' out with him, and I'd see him bring her home and them makin' out in his car in the driveway."

"Did you like her back then?"

"She come home from North Carolina, and she never wanted to see another baseball player or nobody that was like him."

Becky Diane puts her hand back on his thigh. "I know she must be treating you bad."

"I got me some personalized license plates which said PAM-BOB." Bobby holds up his hands as if he held the license plate. "I'd never even asked her out. I just pulled up in her driveway while she was settin' on the porch, so she could see how I felt. She thought I was crazy." He laughs.

"She must have been flattered."

"She married me, didn't she? I been married to her ten times longer than he ever was."

"Would you really marry me if you could?"

"What?"

"You said this afternoon you'd marry me if you could."

Bobby stares at the blank TV. Then he looks over at the kitchen table. "See them things." Piled on the table are *Playboy* magazines, straws, and packets of ketchup and salt. "I stole them things. That's what I did today. I stole them things. And I spared a life."

THIRTEEN

Her feet hurt, and she hopes she can drive home without falling asleep. She pays for a box of McDonaldland cookies to take home to Bobby. Pamela is the last one to leave. It's Monday night, but since it's summer, high school kids are out. A line of cars come from the direction of Starlite Drive-in. Some boys yell at her as they go by in their growling car jacked up on tires about three times too big. She ignores them. A few years ago she would have been flattered. Now she figures boys like that yell at every girl. They would yell at Betty Jo.

She gets in the Maverick and turns the ignition, and it

grinds and grinds and grinds, then stops doing anything. Pamela rests her forehead on the top of the steering wheel. She thinks of the Camaro she saw on TV in Raleigh—years ago. For some reason that she realizes probably doesn't make any sense, she thinks that if she had bought that Camaro she would not be here tonight. She thinks of California, a place she's never been.

The Vampire said he really wanted to sell the Camaro that night. "Make me a reasonable offer," he said. "We're open all night. We don't sleep. We do get tired though, and we sell cars at crazy prices."

Pamela hadn't made any friends in Raleigh. She met another player's wife when she and Lon first got there, but the other wife did nothing but brag about how her husband was probably going to be promoted to the Triple A League soon—while Lon was dropping two or three balls every game.

"Late-night specials. Easy credit. You can be on TV," The Vampire said.

Sitting on her sofa, her legs tucked under her, Pamela thought about her mom—she had thought she hated her mom, but now she missed her—and her girlfriends back home in Ohio (although a lot had also gotten married and moved away) and all the boys who had told her they loved her: seven since she was thirteen.

She reminisced—as if it had been years and not months ago, just that spring in fact—about her and Lon making love in his Skylark. She would hold his face against her breasts and pat his sweaty hair and listen to his breathing and feel her own sweat trickle down her sides and feel herself slipping on the slick vinyl.

"Every pre-owned car has passed the safety-lane inspection."

She kept looking back and forth from the TV to the plastic clock on the wall. Lon was supposed to be back from a road trip that night. The clock was a bright yellow chicken turned sideways. A relative of Lon's gave it to them as a wedding gift.

Parts of the movie had been boring so far. Some male aliens needed women, ones with their minds sucked out. She picked up a copy of *Cosmopolitan* from the coffee table. Looking at magazines and watching TV were pretty much all she'd done since moving to Raleigh. In the mornings, she watched Phil Donahue and reruns of "I Love Lucy" and "The Beverly Hillbillies" and game shows. When the noon news came on, she changed the station and watched four soap operas. She looked àt *Redbook, People, Cosmopolitan,* and *Vogue.* At night, if the Rebels were playing at home, she had to go to the games. When the team was on the road, she fixed a TV dinner or a pot pie and begin the evening by watching "The Newlywed Game," wondering how she and Lon would do. Then things improved because prime-time started. Then late, if she couldn't sleep, The Vampire was on every night.

She had stopped fantasizing, when she looked at the pictures of beautiful women in beautiful clothes in the fashion magazines—had stopped fantasizing about being able to look and dress like them some day soon, had stopped fantasizing about Lon being in the major leagues, making a million dollars a year. She had stopped imagining that future because Lon was hitting one thirty-five and dropping balls like hot potatoes. In the home games Pamela had gone to, Lon looked so clumsy playing third base she was reminded of a retarded boy she knew back in Ohio.

In high school, Lon seemed to float or glide around the bases after hitting balls so hard they almost instantly vanished. And there was the way he could crouch behind home plate—he had been a catcher in high school—for the longest time; his leg muscles were incredible.

All that grace and power—gone. Pamela wondered whether he might have suddenly gotten a brain tumor or something.

"These quality cars have been completely reconditioned

by our trained mechanics. Drive your car off the lot and all the way to California. Worry free, I guarantee."

She was sleepy, but she didn't want to sleep. "How would I get there?" she said aloud and realized she was talking about The Vampire's car lot. "Go to hell," she said to the clock. She could call a cab.

"Stay tuned for tonight's second feature, one of my favorites, *The Three Stooges on Mars.*"

She closed her eyes and saw herself getting dressed—jeans, blouse, shoes—then standing at the kitchen counter with a pencil and a pad of paper with yellow daisies along the bottom of each page, wondering whether she should leave a note.

Or tell him on TV. What would she say? "How would I get there?" And she realized she was talking about California.

She awoke, startled, a vampire on the TV, and she shouted, "Mom!"

She awakes, her forehead sore from where it's been resting on the steering wheel. She looks at her watch.

She groans getting out of the car. She slams the door, then brings her fist down on the roof, but there's only a dull, soft thud. And she unlocks the McDonald's and uses the phone to call her mother.

FOURTEEN

Lon hopes the beers will make his headache go away and give him some energy. He tries reading the encyclopedia, but the words keep blurring. When he turns on the TV, he feels he's had a bit of luck. On channel three out of Huntington, West Virginia, the Reds are on, playing the Mets. Pete Rose is getting closer to Ty Cobb's record nearly every day. When Rose comes up to bat, Lon shouts, "Go, Pete!" at the TV, the way he did when he was a kid.

He usually tries never to think about his summer playing for Raleigh, but after the Reds score a bunch of runs and he's feeling good—the day's not turning out so badly after all—he lets himself reminisce about one good moment, the time he hit his only home run as a professional baseball player.

The score was tied, and he hit the ball to the right field corner, where it took a funny bounce off the wall, off the huge face of a pretty girl drinking a Dr Pepper. The outfielder slipped, trying to get to it. As Lon ran toward third, the third-base coach pointed to home plate and yelled, "Home, Lon! Home!"

But then the bad memories pour over him, and he lies face down on the sofa. The Rebels ended up losing the game, partly because Lon bobbled a ball hit to him at third base. Why did they have to make him play third base? He was a catcher, had been a catcher ever since Pee Wee League. They said they didn't need another catcher; they needed a third baseman. That's probably what Johnny Bench was told, near the end of his career, his knees giving out. The one year Bench played third base, he was the worst third baseman in the league, Lon remembers. But Bench had always been the best catcher. Same damn thing happened to Lon. Best to the worst. Same damn thing. He always felt out of place at third base, never comfortable. Always felt like one leg was shorter than the other. Felt like the glove he wore wasn't his. And it wasn't. His was a catcher's mitt.

They said they were mainly interested in his hitting. But he couldn't hit. He dropped balls, made wild throws—and he couldn't hit.

He was suddenly a failure.

And being a failure was as mysterious to him as being a success had been. Hitting a baseball had come naturally; he could never explain it. He never thought about it. Then in Raleigh he thought about it all the time, the position of his feet, the angles of his elbows; people gave him advice, which didn't help.

All his life he had thought the hills, farm land, and small towns of where he grew up were dull and ugly, but that summer in the South, he yearned to be back there and to be back in high school, which he had just left. In his mind, Ohio was all freshness and lushness; it was heaven compared to Georgia, Alabama, the Carolinas, and Florida— the redneck towns' ramshackle ball parks with tacky billboard pictures on all the outfield walls so that a baseball coming into the plate from the pitcher's mound got lost in the tooth of a smiling girl who used some goddamn special formula toothpaste.

DRINK COKE. JOHNSON'S HARDWARE. VALLEY FORD.

Fuck them all.

One thing he felt he was learning was that only the present counted. Only in the present did you feel some thrill, some pleasure, or some pain. Memories didn't do you a damn bit of good.

He sits up on the sofa. He should get to work, he tells himself:

Fix the tractor.

Mow the fields.

Repair the fences.

Paint the house.

In a few minutes he stands up and goes to the back door and looks out. Then he walks to the barn. The big door is heavy and hard to open. Inside, it smells the way it did years ago. Hay and manure. The ghosts of pigs and cows and chickens are everywhere. The red and gray 1947 Ford tractor sits in here. By the door are an old baseball and a bat.

He takes them outside and swings the bat a few times at imaginary fast balls down the middle of the plate. Then he drops the bat and tosses the ball above his head and makes basket catches bare handed. "Willie Mays," he says aloud. He tosses the ball as high as he can, and it sails behind him and comes down on the roof of the barn. While it skates down the roof, he runs to the side of the barn to catch the ball when it drops from the overhang.

When he comes back to the front of the barn, a little red car is turning into the driveway. Clutching the ball, he runs to the house, slams the door, and locks it. He goes into his room and sits under the window, breathing hard. He hears the car crunching the gravel. When it stops, he peeks out. A Chevette. There's a knock at the front door. Then another. After a couple of minutes, he hears footsteps going around the house.

He glances at the open closet and notices his stack of *Playboys* is gone. "What the hell?" he whispers and looks around. Nothing else seems to be missing. He thought for sure he saw that stack of *Playboys* in there only yesterday. He knows he did. He lifted one and looked at the cover for a second, then put the newspapers—newspapers about him—back on top of the magazines. So . . . ?

"Lon!" he hears Cindy call. "Lon!" He sits still. "Lon!" She's looking all over for him. "Lon!" Her voice is drifting off toward the barn.

Lon wants to stand up and holler, *Go away!* But if he does, he knows she won't. She'll want to talk. She'll ask him questions. *What's wrong? Did I do something? What about last night?*

Jesus, last night.

There he was like some damn kid—at the drive-in movie, in the back seat, sucking on a young girl's nipples. She said she wouldn't go all the way. "I'm jail bait for you, old man," she said. She kept resnapping her jeans.

They were drenched in each other's sweat. Strands of her hair kept getting in her mouth and his. There were beer cans and oil cans on the floor of the back seat, old oily rags, a McDonald's bag full of garbage. "I'm not dumb enough to let myself get pregnant," she said.

Jesus. Jesus H. Christ. Just like high school. They almost always gave in eventually. Especially if you pulled a rubber out of your wallet and told them you loved them. Cindy, though, just wanted to French kiss and pull on his dick.

Finally, he came all over his jeans and her hand. And a

fog lifted, and a cold draft slid up his spine, and he was mad. But at the same time, he was glad he hadn't done anything to her. He was tired as hell.

"Lon! Lon!"

He peeks out again, and she's standing by the driver's door of her Chevette, about ready to give up.

Lon looks at his closet again.

FIFTEEN

Pamela and her mother are at the kitchen table, drinking coffee.

"You're gettin' crow's feet around your eyes already. You want a bottle of Oil of Olay? I got about twenty bottles when West Union Drugs had their going-out-of-business sale. You remember that? About three years ago, not long after your dad passed away?"

"Mom, I'm trying to talk serious here."

"I know, hon. I was just noticing those crow's feet, and I thought to myself, 'She really is unhappy.' "

"I don't want to live with Bobby any more."

Ruth stands up and takes her coffee cup over to the sink. She runs water and rinses the cup, then hangs it on a mug tree. "Who told you?" she says with her back to Pamela.

"Told me what?" Pamela asks, annoyed, thinking her mother is talking about something that has nothing to do with her and Bobby. She rubs the table cloth with her finger tip. It feels greasy and has the smell of new plastic. Pamela remembers sitting here and cutting out paper dolls. She remembers coming home from dates and finding her mother sitting at this table in the dim light, looking up from a magazine and smiling a phony smile, giving her the once over for undone buttons, wrinkled blouse, flushed face. Now her mother looks for wrinkles in her face. "Told me what?" Pamela says again.

Ruth comes back to the table and sits down. "About Bobby. You mean you don't know?"

"Know what?"

"Well, they always say the wife is the last to know."

"Who's he fooling around with? Jeez, he doesn't even have a job."

"Becky Diane Walters. That girl that works at the drivers license bureau."

"But she's *ugly*. Ugly as sin. She's so ugly she could be on television."

Pamela's mother gets a sad look in her eyes, and Pamela thinks about her father. He got cancer and smelled up the house for months, but when he died, Pamela's mother was as hysterical as a woman who loses her husband suddenly, in an accident or at the hands of a crazed killer.

"I'm sorry, hon, about Bobby doin' this to you." Then Pamela's mother surprises her. "You shouldn't give him up to her. If he really cared for her, he'd have left you."

Pamela shakes her head hard. "But, Mom, I don't want him."

"Maybe that's what he senses. Maybe that's why he went to another woman to seek satisfaction. Did you refuse him bedroom privileges?"

"Bedroom privileges?"

"The only thing she's got in common with you is she's a woman."

"No, Mom. You don't see. He's been playing around with this gun he bought, and he acts like a child half the time. I can't rely on him for anything, and I don't think he's ever going to get a job."

"I thought he was always real sweet to you."

"Well, he was in some ways. Sometimes. Sometimes he's all right." It's true. Sometimes he laughs out loud at the TV, has supper ready for her when she gets home from work, and gives her gifts—cute stuffed rabbits and mice and bears; a coffee mug with "Superwife" painted on it.

"He ever hit you?"

"No. But he aims that gun at me."

"When it's loaded?"

"No, but still. . . ."

"He's just playin' then."

"What? He could kill me." Pamela blows out a long stream of air and feels her face flood with hot blood. "Why are you defending him?"

"I just don't think you ought to rush into another divorce. Now I didn't say a word when you left Lon after only a few months."

"I didn't know you liked Bobby so much."

"It's not a matter of me likin' him or not likin' him." Her mother looks toward the window sill where a plant sits. "I gotta remember to water my vines."

"Mom."

"Hon, you're twenty-four years old, and you've been married twice already."

"I know, Mom. Mom, I've been trying. I wanted it to work. I feel like something must be wrong with me. But I just don't know what to do."

"Well, you can't keep gettin' married all the time."

"You don't have to worry about that."

Pamela's lying upstairs in her old room when the phone rings down in the kitchen. The furniture in her room is white with blue trim, and all her old dolls are on shelves her father built. Her father was the only man who ever entered this room. She always told her brother she'd kill him dead if he ever set foot in here.

"Pam!" her mother calls from the bottom of the stairs.

"Yeah."

"That was Bobby again. I told him you were asleep."

"Okay."

It's Pamela's day off, so she doesn't have to deal with McDonald's today. She wonders whether Lon has stopped by there. All day yesterday she expected to look up and see him.

An image comes to her: Lon sitting on the sofa like a zombie in their apartment in Raleigh. He wouldn't talk. He just stared. At nothing.

Once, she picked up one of her *Vogue* magazines, threw it at him, and yelled, "Stop feelin' sorry for yourself and *do* something. You feel *so* bad. For God's sake," and she paused, not wanting to go on but knowing she would. "When you dropped that ball today, I heard some bald man in front of me say, 'Don't he look like a retard?' How do you think *I* feel?"

Lon got up and slapped her.

He never hit her again, but he'd throw lamps, chairs, and knicknacks. When Pamela yelled at him to stop, he'd say, "I'm just tryin' to *do* something, bitch!"

But if his father called, Lon would say, "Everything's fine. I got a cold, but I'll get over it." Then his father would want to talk to her, and she'd have to pretend, too. Toward the end of the summer she left whenever Lon's father called. "I am not here," she would mouth to Lon, as soon as he said, "Hi, Daddy," and she'd walk to the drug store and buy something little, cotton balls or toothpicks or Band-Aids.

Every morning when Lon was not on a road trip, he reached for her and said, "I'm sorry, babe. I love you. I'll be okay."

At the end of the season when he was released by the team, he said to her, "I need you more than anything in the world."

But by then she had made up her mind.

Fits of violence. Fits of crying. Fits of love. She was sick of them all.

SIXTEEN

Ruth watches Johnny Carson as she leafs through the August *Ladies' Home Journal* and sips a Pepsi (a real one, not a diet one), which she knows she shouldn't have, considering the weight she needs to lose, but it's a small pleasure and sometimes small pleasures seem to be all that hold her together. Like now. Pamela is upstairs in her old room, determined to leave another husband.

Ruth usually doesn't stay up this late, but she can't sleep. She wishes Pamela could have at least picked another time, waited a month or two or something. Ruth hasn't gotten over her son, Darrell, leaving for the Army. He just graduated from high school in May. She tried to talk him out of joining, told him about Uncle Ibra, who was killed in World War II and Cousin Ellen's boy, who died in Vietnam. But the Army had those commercials on during the ball games and "Saturday Night Live" and on MTV, which Darrell could watch about six hours straight like some kind of zombie. "There ain't no war, Mom," he kept saying.

If Glen were alive, he would have said, "What the hell else is the kid going to do?"

The house still smells of Glen's cigarettes. At least Ruth *thinks* she still smells them. Maybe she'll ask Pamela whether she smells them, too. When Ruth sees an actor in a movie set in the fifties or sixties with a pack of cigarettes rolled up in the sleeve of his tee shirt, she thinks of Glen because he used to really do that. When they rode around in his Mercury and she leaned against his shoulder, he'd say, "Goddamn, don't smash the smokes."

Sometimes Ruth thinks she hears Glen snoring or coughing and looks toward the bedroom, then remembers he's dead.

The day she married him, in the receiving line at the church, her mother whispered to her, "You're a fool."

Well, maybe she was. She was only sixteen, but she made the best of it. She and Glen stayed together. Now days, she thinks, everybody gets divorced at the drop of a hat. She and Glen had their rough times, a lot of fights even the first year.

Glen fixed cars and talked about becoming a race-car driver. He came home to their little shack of a house with engine oil gleaming on his face and his eyes flashing in the sexiest way. He had sideburns like Conway Twitty's, and he was horny every minute of the day. That was nice. But then there'd be some fight. He'd say her cooking tasted like shit and that he'd rather have TV dinners, or she'd ask him to help with a load of laundry and he'd say, "Are you crazy, woman?" or he'd want to go out with some couple Ruth thought were trash. Or they fought about money. They always fought about money.

But they got through it. They stayed together. Even the times she suspected him of seeing another woman.

At midnight, just as Johnny Carson is introducing somebody she's never heard of, Ruth goes out to the porch and looks up the street, then beyond the house across from hers, the house Bobby grew up in, and sees mountains. She says a prayer for her daughter and Bobby.

Bobby grew up right over there with just his mother—there were all kinds of stories about his father: he was dead; he was in prison for life; he'd run away with a teen-age girl. Four years ago Bobby's mother married an old man who was about seventy-five (she was maybe fifty at the most) and moved to Cleveland.

Bobby wasn't a bad boy. He's not a bad man either, Ruth is certain. Pamela is hard on men.

Ruth looks up the street again, then at her watch, the way she did when Pamela went out on dates. Maybe she was too hard on Pamela back then. She was always acting like some old woman when she was only thirty-three, thirty-four years old. Back then, when Pamela was in high school, Ruth sometimes realized she acted like her own goddamn mother. She interrogated Pamela about dates and friends and said things to her like, "You better start worryin' about something besides what you see in that mirror, girl."

But Ruth was looking in mirrors a lot herself. It was a bad time, one of the times Glen might have been seeing someone, the time Ruth came closest to walking out. "I'm a mess," she would say to her reflection, leaning toward it and touching her face with the tips of her fingers. She was thirty pounds overweight (and still is) and half consciously made her appearance worse by wearing polyester clothes from K-Mart, as if she'd decided that better clothes would be a waste of money on a body like hers. If she had worn flower-print dresses and had had short hair in tight curls, she would have looked just the way her mother did when Ruth was sixteen and crazy about Elvis Presley because he looked so nasty and so sweet. She used to cut pictures of him out of magazines and hide them in a drawer under her panties and bras.

Seven, eight years ago—a bad time.

She'd stay up late, like tonight, unable to sleep, maybe waiting for Pamela to come home from a date. Glen would be snoring his head off. She'd look in their bedroom at him sprawled on his back, his big belly sticking up above the rest of him, the sheets in a pile on the floor because he always kicked them off.

One night, waiting up for Pamela, she went into the bedroom and lay down on her side and gently shook Glen and said, "I love you." He opened his eyes for a moment and stared at her, then rolled over onto his side. "I love you," she repeated.

A harsh cough exploded from deep in his throat. "What the hell?" he muttered. Then he sucked in a long snore.

She sat up, and she realized it didn't matter—she didn't mean it when she said she loved him. At least, not at the moment. Love came and went. That's what she had learned in seventeen years of marriage.

His back was broad, strong looking, somehow cruel looking, but he never hit her, not once. The women on either side of their house had been hit by their husbands, they had told Ruth. The woman in the tacky pink house on the corner called the sheriff on her husband one time, making a scene for the entire street to see. Sometimes she wished Glen *would* hit her. She wasn't sure why. Anyway, she didn't want to think about such a crazy notion.

Glen didn't hit her, and Bobby hasn't hit Pamela. Pamela should be thankful, Ruth thinks. Pamela said Lon hit her.

Ruth never did like him. He had a head so big he couldn't fit it through the front door. He used to sit out front in his old car and honk his horn. Rude.

When Pamela started dating Lon, Ruth started going into Pamela's room when she was out, entering cautiously, as if booby traps might be set. She sweated. She was careful not to disarrange things. She opened drawers, gingerly lifted socks and bras. If she had found something, she would have died, she told herself.

Found what? Drugs? Birth-control pills? A flask of whiskey?

Snooping reminded her of things God hated—the things she grew up feeling guilty about: everything from wearing eye liner to cussing.

She looks up at the stars and lets her breath out slowly. The moon is full. Ruth wonders how many nights have been exactly like this—the temperature around eighty, the stars shining, crickets singing, that smell of grass and trees? It could be a night ten years ago. Twenty. Twenty-five: Elvis singing a love song, the taste of Rolling Rock beer on Glen's lips.

It's just funny, the way the weather is the same, as if it should have changed along with everything else. Maybe when she gets older, she'll convince herself it has—like her Aunt Marie, who claims she remembers when it regularly snowed three feet at a time in the Ohio Valley.

Ruth goes inside her house and presses the buttons on the cable box to find something to watch. She ends up with MTV. Sometimes it hypnotizes her, although she doesn't like many of the songs or musicians. She does like Bruce Springsteen, though. He reminds her a little of the way Glen was when he was young.

She feels a pain in her chest and belches. That slut Madonna is on. Ruth feels awfully lonesome.

She looks toward the bedroom as if she were going to see Glen lying in there. "He's dead. Remember that," she says.

During that bad time—seven, eight years ago (has it really been that long?)—she was always lonely. Surrounded by Glen, Pamela, and Darrell, but always alone. She got a little crazy. She thought she was in love with her dentist.

Dr. Scott was a tall distinguished looking man who had gray temples and who always had liquor on his breath. Once, as he was leaning over her, peering into her mouth, he told her she had beautiful eyes—so large and so green. She felt her face burning. She started having dreams about him.

She went to him every month with some phony complaint. Once, she took him a plate of chocolate-chip cookies. While she sat in the waiting room, she noticed on the wall, among the pictures of animated teeth and smiling children holding tooth brushes, a picture of a cookie with an X drawn through it. Then Dr. Scott came in and said hello. She told him the cookies she held were not hers; they belonged to a friend; she was just taking them somewhere for her. . . .

When she had some little bit of surgery done and Dr. Scott put her to sleep, she woke up with the sensation that her breasts had been fondled. She tried to tell herself she was just fantasizing.

One night while she waited for Pamela to come home from a date, she wrote love letters to Dr. Scott, which she destroyed, burned on the stove top, after reading over once.

Then she heard a car in the driveway, and she hurried out to the porch. As she stood there peering at Lon's Skylark, she realized her robe was open, and she pulled it closed and tied the belt.

She couldn't see Lon or her daughter until Pamela opened the passenger's door and the car's interior light came on. Lon's face looked gruesome in the pale light; long shadows seemed to hang from his eyes.

As Lon backed out and then roared away, Pamela came very slowly up the walk, not looking at her mother, up the steps to the porch and into the yellow light.

Ruth said, "Did you have a nice time?"

"Why are you out here?"

"I was just getting some air. That TV is enough to make anybody feel like they're choking."

"The TV's not on."

"I just turned it off," she said as she took Pamela's bare forearm. Although Pamela resisted for a moment, Ruth led her over to the porch swing and made her sit down. They sat close, and Ruth studied her daughter, who stared at the street. Ruth leaned toward her, looking her over carefully, sniffing at her, as if she could pick up the scent of male hands.

SEVENTEEN

It starts pouring down rain in the afternoon, and the lightning knocks out the electricity. Bobby wakes up when the air conditioner goes off, the fan making a rattling noise as it slows down. The trailer is dark. "Pam?" Bobby says. All he hears is rain on the roof.

He gets off the sofa and looks out a window. Then he takes off his shirt and socks, dropping them on the floor, and goes into the bathroom and gets the shampoo. It's yellow shampoo with two percent egg, the cheapest K-Mart sells.

Outside, Bobby bows his head and gets soaked. Thunder cracks nearby. His jeans get heavy with water. Then he steps under the eaves of the trailer and lathers his head. He likes the smell of the shampoo, and he likes the smell of the rain. He likes the way rain water makes his hair thick and soft.

He steps out from under the eaves and bends over, letting the rain rinse his hair. It starts to hail, and he feels little needles all over his back and head. He sees small hailstones gathering around his feet. Then it's just rain again, and he goes back inside the trailer and dries his hair with a towel and takes his jeans and underpants off.

In the bedroom, he looks at himself in the full-length mirror on the closet door. The closet is across from the bed so you can watch yourself while you screw.

When he and Pamela looked at trailers, he noticed that most of the new trailers had a lot of mirrors in the master bedrooms. Red wallpaper and big mirrors. A couple of trailers had mirrors on the ceiling over the bed. At first, Pamela didn't like the mirror on the closet door because it made her feel funny, she said, like she was on TV or something.

When they first got married, they never missed the TV show "Dallas." They called each other Mr. Ewing and Mrs. Ewing because the characters Pamela and Bobby Ewing on the show were deeply in love. Pamela got tired of the show after a couple of years, but Bobby kept up with it for another season. Pamela would sit at the kitchen table and write letters to friends who had moved away, but occasionally, she'd nod toward the TV at a new character and say, "Who's that?"

The electricity has come back on, and Bobby tosses his wet clothes in the dryer. The dryer turns the whole trailer into a steam bath. He and Pamela haven't been using it much the past year because the washing machine broke down. Pamela's been taking the laundry to her mother's to do. It's a lot cheaper than buying a new washer or going to the laundromat, and her mother helps her.

Bobby thinks his and Pamela's sex life has been hurt by the break down of the washing machine. When the washer went into its spin cycle, the whole trailer shook. Bobby got into the habit of turning on the washer, even if it was empty, when they were about to have sex. It was like having a Magic Fingers machine built into their bed. Bobby got good at adjusting the washer and timing the progress of his and Pamela's sex.

Still naked, Bobby goes into the spare bedroom and looks at his antique toys. He likes handling them and thinking about how kids played with them long before he was born, how they grew up in worlds a lot different from his, how they are really old now or dead, and that's kind of weird for some reason.

He used to have a sign up by the highway saying AN-TIQUE TOYS FOR SALE, but the mobile-home park manager made him take it down. She's a short, chunky woman with short hair streaked black and gray, and she has a bald spot on the back of her head. It looks like somebody puts a bowl on her head and cuts her hair with shrub shears. She's a nasty old bitch, and Bobby thinks somebody ought to blow her away.

He gathers up some of the old toys and carries them into the living room and puts them by the front door. He makes several trips. Then he gets dressed and combs his hair. It's soft and thick.

Outside, the sun is shining. There are puddles everywhere, and birds are all over, catching worms. Bobby puts the toys in the trunk of his Dodge and drives into West Union and is waiting at the courthouse when Becky Diane gets off work. He shows her what he has in the trunk.

"What are you going to do with them?"

"I'm going to give 'em away."

They drive across the Ohio River into Kentucky.

"Why are you going to give them away?"

"I just got to thinking about how a lot of poor kids don't have toys to play with."

"You're sweet, Bobby. But aren't those toys worth a lot of money?"

"Yeah."

"Well, can you afford to just give them away like this?"

"I'm going to get a job."

"Where? Do you have one lined up?"

"Not yet. But I'll get one. I got to. She didn't come home last night."

"Your wife?"

"Who else?"

"Do you know where she is?"

"She went to her mom's house."

"It really is nice of you to give your toys away." She lays her hand on his knee.

"I always have felt sorry for people that don't have."

"That's—"

"Like you."

Bobby pulls onto a dirt road, and in a minute they're in the middle of a cluster of shacks, the hamlet of Sadiesburg. Little dirty kids with long stringy hair are playing in the road. Bobby pulls over, gets out, and opens the trunk.

"Hey, you kids. I got some toys for you."

They gather around, slowly. The adults stand in the doorways of the shacks, their eyes narrowed and their arms crossed. Becky Diane stays in the car and rolls up the windows.

A man steps out onto his porch and spits a stream of tobacco over the porch rail.

Bobby starts handing out toys, smiling. Right away, a boy says, "This ain't nothin' but junk," and spits.

A girl says, "Ain't you got no *new* toys?"

Bobby says to her, "See, honey, these are real special toys. You could sell 'em some day and get a lot of money for 'em."

He touches the girl's shoulder, and she jumps back. "Don't!"

The man on the porch spits another stream, then says, "We don't need none of your junk, boy."

Bobby dumps the rest of the toys on the ground and gets in the car.

"What those kids say?" Becky Diane asks.

Bobby drives away fast, kicking up big clouds of dust.

"Did they thank you?"

"They didn't say nothin'."

"What's wrong?"

"Nothin'."

"What they say?"

"Shut up."

"What's the matter, darling?"

"Shut up."

They're quiet for a minute.

Then Becky Diane says, "Forget your wife. She doesn't deserve you."

Bobby pulls off the road into a ditch full of high grass. The car is slanted way sideways. Bobby takes hold of Becky Diane and kisses her and squeezes her breasts. A pickup truck goes by.

"Bobby, it's broad day light."

"I don't care."

"I'm afraid the car's going to tip over in this ditch the way you got it."

"It won't."

Another pickup truck comes by. It slows down. An old farmer takes a look, and Bobby gives him the finger.

"Let's wait till we get to your place."

"No," Bobby says, getting off her. He starts the car. "I got some things to do. I'll drop you off at the courthouse."

When he gets home, he calls Pamela's mother's house, and her mother tells him Pamela went out.

"Think she'll be sleepin' again next time I call?"

"I don't know, Bobby. I wouldn't push her right now if I was you. Let her think about things."

"Tell her I'm comin' over to see her later tonight. Tell her I love her."

"I'll give her the message."

It's a little after seven in the evening. Bobby gets his .22 pistol out and loads it and walks out to the woods behind the trailer park. Three boys about ten years old are playing back there, and he tells them they'd better stay clear, but he lets them watch him shoot at the cake pan. He wonders whether Pamela is out somewhere with Lon. He hits the pan every time.

"You're good, mister," says one of the boys. "Can I try?"

"This is a dangerous thing. You better not."

"You ever shoot birds?"

"Nope. I happen to like birds."

"I bet you could hit birds if you shot at 'em."

Bobby squints at the kid, lets his head fall sideways, and says, "I know I could."

EIGHTEEN

After working on it a full day, Lon gets the tractor started. For the next couple of days, he mows fields, repairs fences, and slaps paint on anything that needs it. At night he drinks beer, reads the encyclopedia, and watches TV. He's glad he doesn't have a telephone.

Cindy comes by three times. He hides twice, once in the hay loft of the barn; the other time he runs back into the woods. The third time, he has gone into Peebles for paint and motor oil. She leaves him an apple pie from the bakery section of the Kroger supermarket, along with a note saying, "I just thought you might like this. Maybe I'm wrong. Love, Cindy."

Lon can't make up his mind about whether he should see her again. She's a nice-looking girl. But she's not as pretty as Pamela was in high school or still is probably. He didn't get that good a look at her when he went by the McDonald's the other night. He has never had a woman or girl as pretty as Pamela, although he's had his share of good-looking ones. He should go to see her at McDonald's. Then he won't have to fool with Bobby. But showing his face to Pamela isn't easy. She might hate his guts for all he knows.

He thinks sometimes that letting himself lose her was the biggest mistake of his life, but when he had her, he was always wanting other women. He loved Pamela, but he had to be realistic, practical, he used to tell himself when he was a baseball star. He figured that after he made it to the majors he wouldn't be the same man she married, the same farm boy who loved baseball and dreams; something would happen to him. He wouldn't divorce her, but she would have to give him a certain amount of freedom. He often fantasized about nameless models on the covers of women's magazines he saw in grocery stores and about women in *Playboy*; he liked to conjure up images of some actresses on TV. He might meet some of those women some day, and nobody could say what might happen.

He would smile at pretty girls, wink, strut, and say, "You're lookin' mighty fine, honey."

He loved the way they giggled. He could tell from a girl's giggle whether she would let him have her. He had good instincts. He just knew, the way he knew how to hit a baseball—until he lost his instincts in Raleigh. All that summer in North Carolina, when he saw a pretty girl, he blushed and ached deep inside in a way he'd never known before.

And he actually let Fred Potts, a teammate, talk him into going to a whorehouse. They were on the team bus going back to Raleigh, and the inside of the bus was dark and quiet, silent as death because the Rebels had lost twelve of fifteen games on the road trip.

Lon stared out the window at the black sky and the blacker houses and trees and barns. Fred Potts, who was sitting directly behind him, broke the silence when he started singing: "I get off on fifty-seven Chevys, I get off on screamin' guitars." Potts was thirty-four. Lon had heard that Potts played in the majors for three weeks once, years ago. In the game that day, he had doubled and dropped a ball. Lon had dropped two.

Somebody told Potts to shut up.

He stopped singing but hollered, "Boys, we all need to take a little road trip. Out to a whorehouse I know." Potts waited for responses but got none. So he sang again: "If I told you you had a beautiful body, would you hold it against me?"

Somebody yelled, "Fuck you, Potts."

"Yeah, now you're talkin'," Potts said, then sang, "Had me a girl in Kansas City, she had a scar on her left titty. Had me a girl in Kalamazoo—"

"I said fuck you."

Potts put his hand on Lon's shoulder. "How 'bout it, boy?"

Lon turned his head. "Potts, I haven't seen my wife in two weeks."

"What? You weren't seriously thinkin' of goin' home to the old lady, were you?"

Suddenly, Lon realized that Potts' offer wasn't so bad. Going home and facing Pamela wasn't going to be a party, that was for sure. She had dreams, and he was destroying all of them. He knew she didn't want to hear about his aching teeth and headaches and stiff joints. How one leg felt shorter than the other. He'd gotten three hits on the whole road trip.

"Hey," Potts said, "you know what the difference between a wife and a job is?"

"I think I heard it before, Potts."

"After five weeks, a job still sucks."

"I thought it was 'five years.' "

"Nope. Five weeks."

When the bus reached the ballpark in Raleigh, Lon didn't walk home. Instead, he followed Potts to his car.

While Lon rode in Potts' beat-up Nova, heading for a whorehouse outside of Raleigh, he thought about something the Rebel's manager had said to him that day before the game, which was the worst possible time to say anything to a ball player trying to get mentally ready. Lon realized, Potts' tape deck blasting with some hillbilly's wailing, that whenever somebody started a sentence with, "I'm not saying . . . ," the person was always going to say what he said he wasn't: "I'm not saying you're a bad ball player. . . ."

A slump had to end sometime, Lon told himself. He had hit a couple of balls hard the last two games, but fielders made great plays. His luck was bound to change. Soon, he'd hit one hard, and nobody would catch it; he'd hit a broken-bat blooper, and it would fall in. He'd get used to playing third base. Yes, he'd adjust.

Then the truth swelled in his head and pressed at the backs of his eyes; he gnashed his teeth, and something in his gut pulled loose and sank into his bowels.

Sometimes slumps never ended. Sometimes you didn't get well—you just died.

Potts turned into a dirt driveway. The so-called whorehouse was an old farm house sitting far back off the highway, the grass in the yard high and full of weeds and wild flowers. The headlights of the Nova caught the biggest dead tree Lon had ever seen, a black monster reaching down to take the house in its grasp and crush it. Pigs squealed when the car pulled up to the back of the house.

While Potts banged on the screen door and shouted, "Hey, Sara!" Lon stood several feet behind him, trying to see the pigs he could only hear.

"You woke me up, you son of a bitch," a woman yelled. She stood in the doorway, dim yellow light behind her.

"Did you miss me, baby?"

"It's five extra for waking me up."

"Your sister here?"

"Why?"

"I got a friend."

"Where?"

The porch light came on, illuminating a small patch of yard. Lon stepped into the light and nodded at the woman. Small breasted and pale, she was wearing a green silk robe. Her brown hair hung limp to her shoulders.

"This is Lon," Potts said. "He's a ball player, too. A real superstar and a real stud."

"Come in the kitchen while I see if I can wake up Mary Ann."

When he sat down at the kitchen table, Lon pushed two empty beer bottles away from him and toward Potts and whispered, "There's only two women?"

"How many you need, boy?"

"You said it was a whorehouse."

"House." Potts gestured, making circles with his hands. "Two whores." He pointed at the ceiling.

"They got diseases?"

"Who cares?"

"They raise pigs on the side?"

Potts just looked at his own hands lying on the table.

Sara called from upstairs that they could come on up. She met them at the top of the stairs and told Lon to go to the room at the end of the hall.

"Thank you," Lon mumbled, as Potts and the woman disappeared behind a door.

The house smelled as though it had been lived in by old people; something about it made him think of dust and medicine. He walked slowly, thinking he could leave, take Potts' car, and be home with Pamela in half an hour. He knocked and a woman told him to come in.

Lon stepped into the room and nodded at her, relieved that she wasn't ugly. She was on the bed, stretched out and naked—a thin blond girl about his age with a tattoo of a rose beneath her navel. She yawned and stretched, her breasts trembling, the muscles in her arms and legs defining themselves.

"I'm Lon."

"Oh. Well, what you want me to be?" she drawled.

After the girl turned off the lamp next to the bed, the room was black. She didn't talk. Her breathing was soft. She touched him gently. Lon wondered only for a moment, at the very start, what he'd tell Pamela, not just about tonight but about the last two weeks. The last two months. He had no idea.

The girl raked her fingernails down his back, something one of those cheerleaders at West Union High liked to do.

It was so dark he had trouble for a moment determining whether his eyes were opened or closed. It was black either way.

Then the girl started to whine, and he felt sweat bloom

on his back. Her fingers did a dance.

And he saw a slim, nameless, perfect woman. Then she became a different woman, also perfect. Then another.

NINETEEN

It's always busy between eleven and one, but today the lines seem longer than usual, and Ray's yelling, "Let's move it. Ya'll move like a bunch of cows."

Right after Pamela fills an order for ten cheeseburgers with regular fries and small Cokes for a lady with an army of kids, she looks up and sees Lon standing in her line. She can't remember the last time she had her dream; it's been several days, at least. She hasn't been dreaming at all, she doesn't think. Not since she left Bobby.

A fat woman orders, and Pamela says, "What?"

The woman's face turns red. Pamela always screws up with somebody who will be mean about it. The woman puffs her cheeks out, sighs, and repeats her order. She has long black lusterless hair, and Pamela imagines bugs scurrying around in it. Out of the corner of her eye she sees Lon behind the woman, like a bug coming out of her hair.

Pamela turns around, reaching for burgers and fish, some wrapped in paper and some in Styrofoam boxes that come down narrow slides from the grill area. She crushes a box a little, not meaning to grip it so firmly, but everything feels light and slippery, hard to hold. She puts three boxes and a large Coke on the counter.

The woman glares at the boxes, then glares at Pamela. "I didn't ask for no fish," she says. "I hate fish."

Ray pops his head through the door leading from the grill area and yells, "Hey, you're tryin' awful hard to be stupid today, aren't you?"

The fat woman smiles at him, and he smiles back.

Ray's only a year older than Pamela, and they went to high school together. She hates having to take his crap. Turning to get the correct order, she feels the building tilt. The lights brighten. Thoughts stampede: if they were in high school, she'd ask a boyfriend to beat the shit out of Ray. She takes in a long deep breath. Bosses should always be old men with white hair you naturally feel respect for. Ray tried out for baseball one year in high school and didn't make the team. Pamela was a cheerleader. She used to be married to the greatest baseball player in the history of Adams County. She wants to yell that fact to Ray, and she even gets her mouth open, but then realizes she wouldn't be making much sense.

Lon steps up to the counter. She keeps her eyes on the keys of the register and says, "Welcome to McDonald's. May I take your order?" She smells beer.

"I just wanted to say hi." He belches.

"Your order, sir." She remembers how he can be a real fool when he's drunk.

"My daddy left me his farm."

She looks behind her. Everybody's grabbing at fries and burgers and shouting orders. She turns back and sees her line growing. "You gotta order."

He says something in a soft voice, and with all the noise she can't hear what it is.

Ray's voice, high and strained, yells, "Hey, what's goin' on on number two?"

Lon says something else she can't hear.

"You want a hamburger, okay?" She grabs one wrapped in paper off a slide and shoves it into his hand. "Fifty-five cents, please."

"Don't you want me?" Lon says.

"You're drunk."

"But—"

"Fifty-five cents."

Lon hands her a dollar and turns away. She doesn't try to give him his change.

A farmer in overalls steps up and gives her his order. She loses sight of Lon after he goes out the door and turns, weaving, his shoulders stooped. She looks at the farmer who's staring at her. "What?" she says.

Later in the afternoon when Ray disappears for his rendezvous or whatever, Pamela says to Betty Jo, "I'm leaving. When Ray gets back from screwing his girlfriend, tell him I'm sick. Tell him I puked all over the place. Tell him whatever you want to."

Walking out to the parking lot, Pamela wonders what kind of woman would want to fool around with Ray. He's skinny, bones sticking out all over the place, and has orange hair, the color clowns have. And he has no idea of how to dress. This morning he came in wearing red polyester pants that were too short. When he sat down, she could see his shins above his droopy brown socks. She imagines a fat pasty-looking woman, somebody like the fat woman with the buggy hair, in a dingy little motel room telling Ray he sure is sexy, to get those red polyester pants off before she tears them off. Fat. Pasty complexion. Or maybe Ray's woman looks like his wife. Frail, flat chested, hairy arms. Ray's wife brags that her husband is *the manager* of McDonald's, as if that were some prestige job: chief of surgery. Hell. Chief of fries.

Pamela is driving her mother's Buick. The mechanic at Texaco told Pamela that the Maverick needs about six hundred dollars' worth of work. She would rather just buy a new car. She has allowed herself to fantasize about Camaros and Trans Ams, but she'd be satisfied with a Ford Escort if it ran. She thinks she'll sell the Maverick as junk and get whatever she can for it.

She drives down Highway 33 and just keeps going. She has a full tank of gas, and for a few minutes she thinks she needs nothing else. She can keep going. She can be in Pittsburgh before dark. After about forty minutes she ends up in Portsmouth. She passes the Holiday Inn where she spent her first honeymoon. The sign says, "CONGRATU-LATIONS JUDY AND MIKE." She thinks about going to a movie and feels anger well up because she starts thinking about how she and Bobby have never been able to afford cable TV. A few months ago she said to him, "Everybody else in the world has cable."

"You think those starvin' kids in Africa have cable TV?" he said.

"You're missing the point." She looked at the rusty toy truck he was holding. "You must have rust for brains."

"You got McDonald's grease for brains."

She parks on the street, near a movie theater. She walks up to it and looks at posters advertising the movie currently showing. It's an old theater. She's been in it and remembers water stains on the high ceiling and rips in the plushy seats and big stains on the thick carpet. Elegance gone bad.

When she sees old movie actresses on TV talk shows or in commercials or in made-for-TV movies, she almost cries. She wonders whether they sit around watching their old movies all the time, amazed by how beautiful they *used* to be. She thinks about how she's going to get old, and she can't believe the way her life is turning out, has turned out.

The posters show cars smashing into each other and explosions and the hero and heroine kissing, their shoulders naked.

She recalls the smell of the theater, stale popcorn and something cold, musty. She remembers the beam of light in the darkness and Lon's hot breath in her ear, his fingers exploring her crotch, Clint Eastwood blowing somebody's brains out.

When she saw Lon today, she was surprised by what she felt and didn't feel. He looked different. Washed out, smaller, older. He wasn't anything like the beautiful man or the horrible man of her dream. She remembers she once loved him, but she can't recall what the love felt like. He wasn't frightening either. A few times she had had wild fears of him coming in McDonald's and shooting her. There are always stories like that on the news. She was surprised that he just walked out when she treated him cold. The drunk fool.

She walks down the sidewalk, not paying attention to other people until a teenage boy sitting on the step of a pool hall says loudly, "I want a Big Mac, large fries, and a Coke." She turns at the next corner, walking fast, self-conscious about her McDonald's uniform now. She thinks everybody must be looking at her. Wearing her uniform on the street is like going out in public in pajamas.

Finally, she stops, sweaty, her legs aching. She's by a low concrete wall that separates the sidewalk from the bank of the Ohio River. The river is a couple of hundred feet away. On the other side of the wall, in the mud, are cigarette wrappers and beer cans and condoms.

She looks across the river at Kentucky. Mud and shacks and mountains. She looks up the river, toward Pittsburgh, then down, toward Cincinnati. There are no boats.

She drives toward Pittsburgh. The highway turns north. She sees billboards advertising motels and restaurants in Steubenville. What if she just kept going, disappeared? She thinks of a tabloid headline she saw recently: "ALIENS KIDNAP MOTHER OF TEN. *A mother of ten.* Jesus, living with aliens might be easier, she thinks as she turns the car around and heads for home.

Nearing West Union, Pamela feels lucky that Bobby hasn't come to her mother's house to see her. Lucky—but also disappointed and surprised. She wonders whether he really cares about that ugly woman. Pamela glances at herself in the rearview mirror. Crow's feet.

When she gets into West Union, she stops for gas. Her mother will say something if the tank is empty: *Where in the world did you go? You know how dangerous it is for a girl to drive all over creation alone? You never know who's a maniac. I read that mass murderers are usually smart and handsome.*

After getting the gas, she heads for the mobile-home park. She needs to go to her trailer and get some of her things—makeup, clothes, her radio. She imagines herself carrying those things into an empty apartment with bare white walls, a place where she will live alone. But when she gets to the entrance to the mobile-home park, she can't make herself turn in. She just can't do it. She's going ten miles an hour, and a pickup truck honks, then speeds past her, honking again. She doesn't look over. Picking up speed but planning to turn around any moment, she feels as though she's been away from her home, that crappy little trailer, for a long time.

The tires screech and she turns around in a farmer's driveway. When she passes the trailer park again, she takes a good look. Everything looks somehow different, the trees, the utility poles; the colors of the trailers seem to have faded. Everything looks older, more run down.

Returning home from a long trip, she thinks, you're always afraid you're to find your home ransacked and burned to the ground. The trailer is old and crummy, but it's home.

She ends up all the way back in town and turns around in the lot of the Kroger supermarket. The sun is almost gone. It barely winks above some hills. She heads back toward the trailer park. She has to do it. She has to get her things and face Bobby.

She remembers a vacation she took with her parents when she was nine. As they were pulling out of the driveway, her mother said, "Well, the place will probably be ransacked when we get back." Then four hours later, her mother said, "I wonder if I turned that burner off on the stove. I was heatin' some water for my coffee. I think I did. Well, anyway, we've got insurance. If the house is burned down when we get back, I guess I'll get to buy that new sofa I've been wanting."

Pamela worried the entire trip about her clothes and her dolls and her goldfish. She wouldn't eat much, and at motel swimming pools, when other children talked to her, she'd say, "Your house ever burn down?"

At the end of their vacation, nearing home, she said to her father, "I don't wanta go home."

"Christ, girl," he said, "the whole trip you've been wanting to know when we were going home."

It was true. She had wanted to go home, to see whether it was still there. But now she didn't want to face the ashes. Her charred dolls. Her dead gold fish. As they turned onto their street, she hid her eyes, and her mother said, "What in the world is wrong with you?"

The sun drops behind the hills, and Pamela turns on her headlights. She slows down and puts on her turn signal, although no one is behind her. It occurs to her that she should tell Bobby to get out, that she wants to live there. She can't live with her mother—that's for sure.

Bobby's Dodge is parked next to the trailer. The license plate says PAM-BOB. The first time she saw it was over five years ago. She was sitting on the porch of her parents' house one day in early April, and Bobby's Dodge came down the street, but instead of pulling into his driveway, he pulled into hers. He shut off the engine and sat there. She said hi from the porch and waited for him to get out of his car. He didn't. Pamela looked down the street and saw the Mr. Softee ice-cream truck coming for the first time that year. Not until after she saw the truck did she hear its bell. Two small kids ran out to stop it. Then Pamela looked back at Bobby. She was getting mad—he was *so* weird—and was about to go inside when she noticed his personalized license plate. She liked the fact her name was first.

"Why did you do this?" she said, pointing at the front of his car.

He opened his door, got out, walked around to the front bumper, and pointed. "This ain't no joke. I think you're the most beautiful woman I ever seen."

It's gotten dark suddenly. The night is cool and clear, but the window air conditioner is chugging and dripping. Stars bleed their light across the sky.

Some of the residents of the park are sitting outside on lawn chairs, drinking beer or Cokes. Edna, Pamela's elderly neighbor, is sitting in the circle of light from her porch lamp. She raises her scrawny arm and nods her head. "You and Bobby been on a vacation?"

Pamela just says no and opens the trailer door. She flicks on the light and thinks for a minute that she must be on TV or in a dream. The air in the trailer is icy. A can of gun cleaner sits on the coffee table. The colors of everything are unnaturally bright, like on "Miami Vice." Bobby is sprawled on the floor in a pond of blood, his head blown apart.

TWENTY

Almost as soon as Becky Diane gets to work, the sheriff's secretary, Rita, comes into the license bureau. People have started to line up for their eye tests, but Rita says, "Becky Diane, honey, you got to come with me. Right now. This is real important."

"What's this about?" asks Becky Diane.

"Just come with me."

Becky Diane follows Rita down the hall, noticing how fat Rita's rear end is, and into the one women's restroom in the entire courthouse. Becky Diane has often wondered whether the builders assumed that the only women using the courthouse would be a handful of secretaries, that lawyers were men, judges were men, juries were men, and criminals were men.

Rita says, "Honey, you better lean against the sink cause I got some bad news for you."

Becky Diane figures Rita's going to tell her some gossip about somebody who works at the courthouse. Rita's always the first to know about people's operations or divorces or money problems. "Okay. But I can't stay away. I have people waiting to renew their drivers licenses."

"Now don't you get yourself excited. Just let me tell you the best way I know how." She pauses.

"Yes? Yes?" Becky Diane has always been afraid of getting into trouble at work, although she never has in sixteen years.

"See, the sheriff got a call last evening about . . . an incident."

"An accident?"

"An incident. Well, yes, an accident. Maybe. See, it was about Bobby."

"Bobby who?"

"Your Bobby."

"*My* Bobby?" Becky Diane feels her heart go into a sprint.

"Honey, he killed hisself. Shot hisself through the head. Nobody knows if he done it on purpose or not. Honey, are you listening?"

Becky Diane hears a roaring sound, like a huge seashell placed against her ear. The sink she's leaning against is cold.

"You take the day off. You hear?"

Becky Diane turns around and twists the faucets. The water pressure is weak, and the water merely dribbles out.

"I want you to know," Rita says, "I don't judge people. I say live and let live. I know you must of really cared about him. I know most people around here don't understand that."

"Around here?" Becky Diane looks up from the water and at her reflection in the mirror.

"Honey, everybody in town knows you and him were havin' an affair."

Becky Diane hates the way she looks, hates herself for being ugly, and wishes Rita would stop staring at her.

"Everybody knows?"

"Sure, honey. You and him ran around in broad daylight. What do you expect people to think?"

She doesn't know what she expected people to think. She didn't know they would be spying on her and speculating about her. She never kissed Bobby in public or held his hand. She and Bobby could have been just acquaintances. Or friends. Men and women are allowed to be friends. Aren't they? But, no, everybody assumed something dirty was going on. So what if there was. Those people still had no right to think so.

Then the tears finally come to her eyes and spill down her cheeks, and she looks worse than ever, but what does it matter? she thinks. She notices that the mirror is filthy.

"Honey, I'm goin' down to the bureau and tell all those people they'll just have to come back some other time. Don't you worry about a thing. You hear?"

Becky Diane feels Rita's hands squeeze her shoulders and feels Rita blow a sigh against her back. Then Rita leaves. Alone, Becky Diane looks up at the high white ceiling of the women's restroom.

TWENTY-ONE

Pamela hasn't seen Bobby in a suit since the day they got married. They had a small wedding at the First Baptist Church, which his mother attended regularly. Only a couple of Pamela's girlfriends from high school came. Although they had all graduated just a little more than a year before, most had already moved away to Pittsburgh or Cincinnati or Columbus. The girl who had been maid of honor at Pamela's first wedding had moved to Oregon and never written. Bobby's best man was his mother's boyfriend, George. Some of the guests mentioned to Pamela that they thought it was nice Bobby picked his grandfather to be best man. Pamela didn't bother to try to straighten them out.

Bobby borrowed the suit he wore from a guy he knew at the feed mill he worked at, but the guy didn't come to the wedding. The suit was too big, the sleeves so long only Bobby's fingertips stuck out; the pants legs bunched around his shoes. Standing in the receiving line, he kept having to pull his sleeve up to shake hands. Pamela remembers her father getting a grip on just Bobby's finger tips and Bobby's arm flopping like a dying fish.

When she told her father she and Bobby were going to get married, he said that she would have been better off staying with Lon and helping him through his hard time, and even if he couldn't play professional ball, he could have gone to college (hell, anybody could go to college) and become a high-school coach, and their life wouldn't have been so bad.

Now Bobby's wearing one of her father's suits, a brown one. Bobby doesn't look like himself, even though the undertaker plugged the hole in his head. The undertaker also gave him a haircut and put makeup on him. She's standing by his coffin, a line of people behind her, waiting to take a look. She knows that everyone expects her to take her time, so she stares and stares.

She didn't want an open coffin or even a funeral. She wanted to have him cremated, but her mother said that cremation was a horrible thing and that she certainly hoped Pamela wouldn't stick *her* in a furnace when she passed away.

"Bobby didn't pass away," Pamela said. "More like he blew away."

"You don't know what you feel after you're dead. That's why I object to it."

Pamela and her mother were sitting in Ruth's living room the morning after Pamela found Bobby. The TV was on because Ruth thought it would help them feel things were normal. But she didn't think a soap opera was a good idea, so she had "Love Connection" on. A man was talking about the horrible date he'd had with a woman who did nothing but talk about how rich and good looking all her old boyfriends were. She also went to the restroom every five minutes: "I mean how can you have a conversation with a person who gets up to go to the john when you're in the middle of a sentence?"

Pamela looked away from the TV and said, "You don't feel anything when you're dead. That's what being dead means."

"You know your great-grandmother always claimed her husband came to see her after he died."

Since her mother said that, Pamela has been thinking about ghosts. She doesn't know whether she believes in them or not. When her father died, she didn't give a single thought to ghosts, but if they do exist, she's afraid that Bobby is the kind of weirdo who would want to haunt people.

She looked at "Love Connection" for a minute, then said that Bobby would like being cremated. "Maybe I could do something romantic, like pour his ashes in the Ohio River."

"That river's filthy," Ruth said. "I hear people been catching catfish that have tumors."

"Maybe I'd want to keep his ashes on a shelf in my home."

"I hear they give you a little carton like something you get at a Chinese take-out place. My aunt Ellen had Uncle Doug cremated and kept him in a vase on a coffee table, and one time a visitor used it as an ash tray."

Pamela gave in. "Okay." But she was thinking, *If I cremated him, I could flush the son of a bitch down the toilet.*

Now, as she stands by Bobby's coffin, she feels like crying. She feels sorry for him looking so unlike himself. Her mother said people cry at funerals not for the dead person but for themselves. Sometimes that's true, but Pamela knows she's crying now for Bobby and for Bobby's mother, a short scrawny woman Bobby looked just like. She's standing next to Pamela, and her face is red and wet and rubbery looking. Next to her, his arm around her as if to keep her from falling over, is old George, whose face is wrinkle on top of wrinkle.

TWENTY-TWO

For two days Becky Diane has stayed in her room. She told her mother she has the flu, knowing her mother wouldn't get close to her for fear of catching it. Her mother read somewhere that sometimes when people over sixty get a bad case of the flu their bowels blow up. But every few hours she brings Becky Diane a bowl of chicken noodle soup and some crackers, placing the tray by the door, knocking, then hurrying downstairs.

The only man Becky Diane ever loved or was loved by is gone. The son of a bitch is gone. He loved her mind, her hands, her elegant neck. She is certain he really loved her. He had a pretty wife, but he wanted *her*, Becky Diane.

Gone. "The bastard," she whispers. She has never cursed, but now she hisses words Bobby used constantly. "Dork. Dipshit. Motherfucker."

For two days now: she cries and she cusses and she sleeps. When she wakes up, she opens the door of her room and finds a cold bowl of chicken noodle soup.

TWENTY-THREE

One night in August a storm blows the barn over. Lon hears nails and boards screaming like ghouls in movies. He wonders what his daddy felt when he was lying on the kitchen floor dying. At least his mama had people around her. The house shakes when the barn lands. An atomic blast.

In the morning, he takes a look at the giant wreck. He drives into Peebles and knows there are other pay phones but decides to use the one at the Big Boy Restaurant to call the real-estate agent. He figures the agent ought to know about the barn and can maybe give some advice, but Lon gets an answering machine. He just hangs up.

Lon has come to realize that when he gets depressed, he thinks a woman will make things right. But even if he gets hold of a woman at those times, she doesn't help for long. It's like getting drunk. Still, he can't stop feeling the need and looks around for Cindy. He asks a waitress, and she tells him Cindy has the day off. "I don't think she wants to see you," says the waitress, who is pretty, better looking than Cindy even.

"I never met a female that knew *what* she wanted."

Driving home, he tries to remember what it feels like to

make love to a woman, but it seems he can't really remember except in dreams. Most of the time, he dreams about Pamela. Sometimes Gina, a waitress he knew in Oklahoma. She was older than he was and had hard, defined biceps from carrying trays for thirteen years and scars on her ass where, she told him, her ex-husband, a real bastard, used to bite her so hard she bled. Oklahoma was a void but for Gina. Lon washed dishes and took to wearing a cowboy hat. Wearing his new cowboy hat and nothing else, he would walk around Gina's house, singing "Home on the Range."

"You're not a cowboy," she'd say. "You're a baseball player."

"I'm a cowboy now."

"You're a dish washer."

"Just till I have enough money to buy some cows."

Gina. Her breasts bouncing as she crossed a room, her nipples the color of bruises. Her black hair fanned across a white bed sheet. Her black eyes flashing. Her tongue flicking out to sting him with wet love.

Gina. Spitting on their bed. Her rump swaying as she ran out, shouting back, "Don't be here!"

Sitting on the bed, nodding, her dust drifting from the driveway through the open windows, he put his finger in her foamy spit and raised it to his lips.

She had found out about him and the new cashier at the diner. The cashier was eighteen and had acne, but she let Lon bite her ass.

He goes home and looks around at the mowed fields and repaired fences, at the freshly painted house. He's proud of what he's done. Inside the house, he has hung cheap wallpaper that has vertical stripes and painted the bathroom, and he got the toilet to flush right and not overflow.

He looks at the collapsed barn and wonders whether he can sell the lumber. He needs money. A couple of days ago he sold some rusty parts of old farm machinery to an antique dealer in Mt. Orab over in Brown County. The man said city people would hang the stuff on their walls.

He sits on the sofa, trying to read his encyclopedia, but he keeps thinking about girls he's known: Cindy, Betty, Lois, Kathy, Gina, Debby, Mary Sue, Pamela, Ann, Lori, Jan. . . . He wonders how many women his daddy had in his life. Maybe only one. If Lon could find the right woman. . . . Maybe after he sells the place, he'll go back to Oklahoma. He wonders where he can find Cindy. He wonders whether Pamela is living with her mother—he heard about Bobby.

Later in the afternoon, Lon goes into Peebles again to call the real estate agent and gets hold of him this time, asks what's going on, why he hasn't shown the place, and tells him about the barn. The agent says he's going to put "Make offer" in the newspaper and the real-estate catalogue.

Lon goes to Pizza Hut to eat supper. His waitress is a sweet-looking brunette with a nice smile. She keeps asking him whether he needs anything, but his instincts aren't sending him a clear signal. In any case, he decides he'd better keep his hands off her, or he won't have anywhere to eat. He already has to stay away from McDonald's and Big Boy.

When he gets home, there's a pan of rubber dog shit by the door and a note from Cindy: "Hear you were looking for me. It's nice to know you're thinking about me. I've been thinking about you, too. I've been thinking about how I thought I cared about you. I was wrong."

TWENTY-FOUR

Pamela talks to her baby—"I got us some ice cream, Pumpkin"—after she gets home from the grocery store and lifts the carton out of the bag, as if the baby were not inside her but waiting at home for Pamela's return. Two weeks after Bobby killed himself—nobody could say for sure whether it was an accident or suicide—Pamela found out

she was pregnant. She'd been using her diaphragm without the creme because the cream was so expensive.

Sometimes she forgets about the baby, like when she's
shopping, working at McDonald's, or watching something
exciting on TV. She figures that when she gets bigger she'll
never forget. Then she'll have the baby, and her life will
never be the same.

After she puts the groceries away, she watches "The
Newlywed Game." She says, "That guy's getting old."
She can't believe how old the show's host looks. She
watched the show when she was little and always wanted
to be on it, mostly because she thought the host was in-
credibly cute. Now he's getting gray, and yes, bald, too,
Pamela decides, although he combs his hair to hide it.
Deep lines are etched across his forehead, probably from
raising his eyebrows so much.

"What kind of car," he asks, "will your wives say, gentle-
men, is best for making whoopee in?"

A skinny man with crooked teeth says, "A hearse."
There go the eyebrows. "It's long," the skinny man explains. "You can lay down in it."

"Oh. Okay," the host says. He looks at the camera. The
eyebrows spring up again. Deep lines.

"He used to look a lot different," Pamela says to her
stomach, to Melinda or Matthew. She wants it to be Melinda.

She wonders how many of the couples on "The Newlywed Game" end up divorced. Some of them seem to really
hate each other's guts.

When the show's over, Pamela sits on the porch and
watches the traffic. The one-bedroom house she now rents
is on the main strip of Peebles, close to the street and only
two blocks from McDonald's, a good location since she
doesn't have a car anymore. Her mother wanted Pamela to
live with her, but Pamela told her if she did that she'd
miscarry for sure. Her mother cried. But that was last
month, and her mother has brought over blankets—she

says Pamela will freeze in this house when winter comes—and boxes of canned food to show she cares. Pamela feels a little like somebody on welfare.

Often the cars passing her house are going too fast and change lanes recklessly. "That guy drives like a nut," Pamela says to her baby.

She watches an orange Pinto go by. The driver is looking at her. She almost waves, then realizes it's Lon. In a minute, the Pinto comes past the house again, but Pamela is inside with the door locked, peeking through a chink in the curtains.

Pamela watches a horror movie starring Yvonne Strickland. Yvonne went to West Union High School in the late sixties. When Pamela was a little girl, she heard about how Yvonne moved to California after she graduated, married a rich man, and acted in movies. Yvonne was the closest thing to a celebrity Adams County could claim.

Satan's Touch is about a young woman who sells her soul for eternal youth and beauty. Nobody in the movie can act, in Pamela's opinion, including Yvonne, who has on a miniskirt in most of the scenes, showing off her good fleshy thighs. She has big breasts, too, but Pamela has seen prettier girls around West Union and Peebles; she considers herself prettier than Yvonne, whose blond hair is obviously dyed. Yvonne has on an awfully lot of dark eye shadow. The mole on her cheek looks phony. Pamela doesn't think Yvonne made any movies after the early seventies. Probably got too fat.

When Pamela was growing up, Yvonne was better known in Adams County than any sheriff or mayor or criminal. Nobody had expected anything of her. Nobody noticed her until she showed up in a movie no one would have gone to if Yvonne's mother hadn't bragged to everybody that her daughter had "made it" in Hollywood. Then every girl in West Union claimed to have been a good friend of hers. Boys claimed to have screwed her.

And Pamela thinks about how Lon was famous, too. Everybody predicted he'd be making a million dollars a year by the time he was twenty-five. She thought she'd be married to him forever—they were eighteen, and they would never die.

Then she remembers Lon, that summer in Raleigh, telling his father on the phone that everything was all right. At the time, the lie made her mad; now it seems only pathetic.

Maybe she could have been more sympathetic, more understanding. When she came home from Raleigh, her mother said, "Did you support him the way a wife's supposed to?"

Pamela was sitting in her mother's living room, minding her own business, looking at a *Vogue* magazine. She threw the magazine down and said, "Hell with him. What about *me*?"

In *Satan's Touch*, handsome men fall in love with the woman who has sold her soul. But they die instantly if they lay a finger on her or if she touches them. Pamela can identify—she, too, is bad news for men. Maybe she didn't love Lon or Bobby enough, although she remembers a time in high school when she would have gladly died for Lon. There was a lot more passion with Lon than with Bobby. She recalls sweaty nights in the back seat of Lon's '64 Skylark, the way she felt out of control, always a little surprised, as her heart calmed, at the reappearance of the world: the sounds of crickets, cars in the distance squealing their tires, the rustling of trees. Her lips would swell from so much kissing. No other boy meant a thing to her. Now, there's no one. No man who means anything to her. No interest.

At the end of the movie, Yvonne's character is somehow freed from her contract with Satan, but she immediately ages about two hundred years. A young man who looks slightly like Paul Newman still loves her. He holds her hideous corpse in his arms and cries.

Pamela remembers she found a gray hair in her head

yesterday.

She has to get up at five in the morning to make biscuits at McDonald's. She feels sick and doesn't take a shower. "You go ahead and sleep some more," she says to her stomach. Sometimes she thinks about a movie Bobby took her to when they were dating: an alien from outer space raped a woman, and she gave birth to a monster that ripped its way out of her stomach; the monster was green and had big red eyes and fangs, and it sneered at its mother's bloody corpse.

At work, Betty Jo is already mixing batter for the biscuits. She's brought in her ghetto blaster and is wagging her fat rear around, and Madonna is screeching about feeling like a virgin.

While the biscuits are baking, Betty Jo and Pamela go into the party room, which is furnished with bright plastic tables that look like lily pads and with stools that look like mushrooms, and there's a plastic statue of Ronald McDonald. Betty Jo scratches Ronald McDonald's crotch and says, "That feel good, buddy?" She lights a cigarette and says to Pamela, "You don't look good. You're all pale."

"I'm getting the flu or something. *You* seem to be feeling pretty good."

"It's my birthday. The guy I live with says he's got something for me I'm gonna love."

"Happy birthday."

"Yeah, I'm thirty today. Hard to believe I made it this far. Dirty thirty."

Pamela thought she was closer to forty. "Congratulations."

"Yeah, dirty thirty. Hey, why don't you go on home. I'll tell Ray you're sick."

Pamela stays until about nine-thirty. Then she does leave, feeling achy, her head hurting. The walk home wears her out.

She watches the last few minutes of "Donahue," then

goes into the bathroom to wash her face. She looks in the mirror at her pale face and dirty hair. Dirty thirty, she thinks. For a moment, she can't remember how old she is. Twenty-four. Only twenty-four, she thinks. She hears a game show come on the TV. She thinks she's found another gray hair just when someone knocks at the front door. She takes her time getting it.

Lon is on the other side of the screen door. Pamela looks to make sure it's latched.

"I been meaning to come see you," he says.

"You saw me last night."

"Yeah, I saw you sittin' out here. But you know what I mean."

"Well, what do you want?"

"I'm sorry about comin' in the McDonald's when I'd been drinkin'. I just wanted to be friendly."

"You want to come in?" she says.

"Yeah, sure."

But she makes no move to unlatch the door. She just stands there, staring through the screen at his chest. He's wearing a white tee shirt that says "Van Halen" in screaming red letters.

Lon shifts his weight from one foot to the other. His hands are in the pockets of his jeans. "You don't look good," he says. "You sick?"

"I'm old."

"Hell, we're still kids." He reaches up and combs his long hair out of his eyes with his fingers. "You know they still got my picture in the trophy case at the high school?"

Pamela stares at the dirty pink slippers on her feet. She's wearing an old terry-cloth robe. A voice on the TV shouts, "Come on down!" and an audience applauds.

"Say, you gonna let me in so we can talk?"

She looks at Lon's face. He looks boyish, but when he smiles, nervously, the skin around his eyes cracks.

Then he looks off in the direction of Pamela's neighbor's house, at something Pamela can't see. He says, "I was wonderin' if we couldn't start seein' each other. I mean since Bobby's . . . gone." He waits. He squints at whatever he sees.

"I'm pregnant. Did you know that?" A dump truck rumbling past shakes the house.

Lon looks at her. "No."

"Well."

"Yeah, well. . . ." Again, he shifts his weight from one foot to the other.

She steps back and slowly swings the door shut.

TWENTY-FIVE

Stacked all around her room—on top of the dresser, the small white desk, the night stand, on the floor against the wall, stuffed under her bed—are books. Romances, mysteries, science fiction, and biographies of movie stars. Becky Diane stopped reading when Bobby came into her life. There didn't seem to be time, with meeting him places and talking to him on the phone and thinking about him. She loved to think about him.

Now she's reading again, three or four books a week. But some lunch hours, evenings, and Sunday afternoons, she doesn't feel like reading. Instead, she just wants to remember Bobby. In some ways, thinking about him is better than actually being with him because she doesn't think about the way he was nasty sometimes and the mean things he said about people and the way he would suddenly pull out of her embrace or knock her hand away.

She thinks only about the times he touched her hair or face with the tips of his fingers and said things like, "You got real beautiful hair. And, you know, your hands could be in movies. I saw a woman on TV, and she made movies. Nobody ever saw her face, but her hands had been in twenty movies and a bunch of TV commercials."

She thinks about holding his hand while they sat on the trunk of a fallen tree in the woods, the sun coming through the leaves and dappling the ground around them. They watched squirrels and rabbits and birds. She doesn't remember the way he pointed his finger at them, aiming it like a gun.

TWENTY-SIX

September.

Sitting on the edge of the sofa, leaning toward the TV, Lon sees Pete Rose line a single to left field to pass Ty Cobb's record.

As soon as the ball drops, fireworks go off, and Lon wishes he had a color TV. Now he sees Pete's mom and his young wife, his second wife, who's holding her and Pete's baby, Tyler. The Reds players surround Rose. The older players who have known him a long time slap his back. The younger players shake his hand. Marge Schott, the team owner, a small sturdy old woman, shuffles out to first base and hugs him. The TV announcer says Pete's dad is probably looking down from somewhere above and smiling on his little Petey.

Lon sits back as he watches Schott present Rose with a new Corvette—the excitement suddenly draining from him as it hits him that what Pete Rose has done does him, Lon, not a bit of good. He wonders why anybody cares what a baseball player does. But fifty thousand people in Riverfront Stadium in Cincinnati are still cheering their heads off.

He leaves the TV on, but he goes outside, picking up the old bat and ball by the door on his way out. It's only a few minutes after eight, and there's still some light, a hazy gray.

Lon looks in the direction of the neighbors' place, their shack and their car corpses, remembering those kids he gave his autograph to.

He takes a batter's stance with the bat in his right hand and tosses the ball as high as his eyes, then swings. There's a satisfying crack, and for a moment he sees himself in a filled stadium—his mama and daddy and Pamela sitting in box seats behind home plate.

And the ball sails over the collapsed barn.

TWENTY-SEVEN

Pamela sits on the sofa, watching a game show, her whole body aching. Her belly is swollen, and her thighs are fat. She can press her finger into her calf and leave a dent. The game show's emcee is explaining that people interested in being on the show can write to an address in Hollywood, California.

She sees herself—thin, the top down on her Camaro, the wind whipping back her hair as she speeds across the desert, headed for the ocean.

Then she wonders why she couldn't have met a rich man, like Yvonne Strickland, and lived in California. She knows—as if it were something she had never known before—that she's going to get old. She wonders whether she'll ever be in love again—or believe she is, the way she once believed she was in love with Lon.

Desperate love.

The baby kicks.

VICKI'S PLACE

Herbert met Vicki at The Blue Room nightclub when she was living in Cincinnati with her sister. Now she lives in a trailer park near Dayton. She told Herbert she had to move because her brother-in-law, Ed, kept making passes. When she and Ed were alone in the house, he'd walk around naked, pretending to look for a clean towel. "The linen closet was always full of clean towels," Vicki told Herbert. "Sis is one of these real obsessed housekeepers. She lives to keep clean towels in the house." Naked, Ed would come to Vicki's room and stand in the doorway and ask if she'd seen a clean towel. "He has this beer belly with hair all over it and legs like toothpicks. Some guys suffer from some really incredible delusions. I mean he'd stand there with this grin and his eyes half closed, which I guess was supposed to be sexy. He thought he was giving me a big thrill."

Before Herbert shaves each morning, he stands back from the mirror and takes long hard looks at himself. He sucks in his stomach and sometimes asks his wife, Carol, whether she thinks he's fat. "What I mean is, would you look at me and say, 'There's a fat man?' " He knows he isn't fat, that he just has more of a gut than he used to, but he likes to hear his wife tell him he doesn't look fat at all.

There were two women before Vicki, but he didn't fall in love with them. One was five years older than he was; the other was married and had three small children.

When he and Vicki first got together, they lied to each other about some things. Vicki said she had no kids. Herbert said he owned a bakery and had never cheated on his wife before. By the time they became truthful they'd been to motels a dozen times, and she was buying special underwear, and he had given her three hundred dollars to order three hundred pieces of Santo Gold jewelry—so the lies didn't matter.

*

Steve and his father put their clothes in grocery bags because Herbert doesn't want to take the suitcases. He doesn't want to take anything Carol might need someday. "You never know. You might want to take a Caribbean cruise or spend a weekend in Atlantic City."

Carol bustles around the house, mentioning things they might want to take, showing them things she's found in drawers and cupboards. She bursts out crying only once, and she stops quickly, holding up a sock and saying to Herbert, "This has a hole. I guess you don't want it?"

Herbert takes hold of her shoulders and says, "I hope you can find the kind of happiness I have. I really do."

Steve watches all this. He wants to get going. He's thirteen and doesn't want any of the toys his mother has put in a box for him. He wants just his baseball cards and his glove and the rubber ball he squeezes a hundred times a day to build up his forearms; his father told him that a lot of professional ball players did that when they were teenagers.

In one bag, Herbert puts all the bottles of cologne Carol has given him for Christmas and his birthday over the years. The bottles are shaped like antique cars.

Then Steve and his father stand on the porch, holding their paper bags, and Steve's mother looks at them through the screen door. There are dark crescents under her eyes, and her lips are swollen. Steve can't imagine staying with her. The woman is constantly touching him and talking to him.

"I love you," she says to Steve.

He nods impatiently. "I'm going to take this stuff to the car."

A few minutes later, his father gets in the car. He looks as if all his blood had been drained from him, but he smiles at Steve and says, "You'll like her. And her boy will be a big brother to you."

As they drive toward Dayton, Steve looks out at the landscape. It's a bright fall day, and the leaves have just turned. A couple of times he looks at his father's hands on the steering wheel and hopes his own hands get that big. His father played baseball in college, and Steve thinks of him as a baseball player, although he does other things to make money.

*

Herbert's car is a partially restored '53 Buick. He loved the car when he first bought it, all that chrome and the thickness of the steel and the way the car sat up high above other cars, like a truck. He did a lot of work on it, but things kept going wrong, little things mostly. When the gas gauge stopped working, his interest faded fast.

As he and his son drive toward Dayton, he thinks about the long drive he's going to have to make each day to get to his job in Cincinnati. He's a baker, and he'll have to get up at three in the morning to make donuts. But he's used to not sleeping much. Sometimes he catches a nap after the morning rush and another in the afternoon after work. Some nights he doesn't bother to go to bed.

He used to teach high-school history, but every year the

kids got crazier. He caught them screwing in janitors' closets; he had a kid almost die of an overdose right in class in the middle of a lecture about the Puritans. When somebody on TV talked about how bad America's teachers were, he felt angry and humiliated. He wanted a life with few confrontations and conflicts. He wishes people could just leave each other alone to do what they have to. His job at the bakery is nice because he doesn't have to bother with selling the stuff; he likes making dough into all kinds of shapes. When he taught school, he sometimes thought he'd go berserk and start beating the crap out of the kids.

*

Steve reads the small hand-painted sign next to the door: "Vicki's Place." The words are red and bordered in yellow flowers. Her trailer looks pretty much like the others in the park. They remind Steve of cracker boxes, tin boxes with pipes on their roofs. Some have fake chimneys and fake gables. One has cardboard halloween decorations on the roof, a couple of smiling ghosts and a smiling witch.

Vicki holds the screen door open and says hi. Then Herbert takes hold of it and tells Steve to go on, and Vicki backs away to let him in. She's twisting one of her rings; she has one on every finger.

*

Vicki likes the way Herbert goes right over to Tom, who's sitting on the sofa in front of the TV, and shakes his hand and says, "Tom, I want you to feel free to talk to me about anything any time. I really mean that."

Tom sits there like the sixteen-year-old slug he is, until Vicki says, "Well, aren't you going to say anything?"

Tom looks around at her and then looks up at Herbert, who's standing above him. "So, ah, you're a baker?"

"Yeah," Herbert says. "Now I am. I've done other things." Vicki feels a little embarrassed but doesn't know exactly why. She hopes Herbert will be a good influence on

Tom. She doesn't know what to do with the kid. She and Tom have nothing to say to each other. He makes bad grades in school, but she figures that maybe he's stupid, so why hassle him about it?

Then she looks at Steve and smiles, but she has been hoping that Herbert could convince him to stay with his mother. She hasn't the slightest idea what she's going to do with him.

"I'll get you guys something to drink," she says. But all she finds in the refrigerator are three plastic bottles of flat Coke.

"It's okay," Steve says. "I like flat Coke."

*

Steve thinks Vicki is a lot prettier than his mother. She has slightly frizzy blond hair and is built. The father of one of Steve's friends is always watching TV and nodding at the screen and saying, "*Jesus*, that woman's built like a brick shithouse!" Steve likes the sound of the phrase.

Vicki pours flat Coke into glasses with the Flintstones stenciled on them. "These are the only things my mom let me have when I left home," she says. Steve gives her a little smile; he doesn't know what to say. The glass she hands him has Pebbles on it. His father gets Fred.

Steve, his father, and Vicki stand in the kitchenette. His father just keeps staring at Vicki and grinning. Vicki glances around at the toaster and the fruit magnets on the refrigerator and the grease on the stove top. Then suddenly she says, "Hey, Steve, let's arm wrestle. You like to arm wrestle, don't you?"

They face off at the table in the kitchenette. Her hand is smaller than his and warm. Her fingers are slender and have dangerous-looking nails painted scarlet. "You got a lot of rings," Steve says.

"You know there's nothing like the feel of Santo Gold—pure gold—against your skin?"

Herbert says, "One, two, three, go."

Quickly, she slams Steve's arm to the table, then rolls up the sleeve of her blouse and shows off her small hard bicep. Steve figures she beat him because she's a lot older than he is.

"That's from waiting tables for twelve years," she says and grins. "Carrying those trays." She looks back and forth from Steve to Herbert.

"You're really strong," Steve says.

"Well, I don't wait tables any more." She drops her arm, stands up, goes over to the counter next to the sink, and gets a cigarette out of her purse. "But I still have these damn muscles." Lighting the cigarette, her hand shakes. "Tom. Show Steve here around. Show him where he's going to sleep."

Steve will have a sleeping bag on the floor of Tom's room. On the wall are pictures of professional wrestlers, football players, and boxers cut out of magazines. An old Teddy bear with its eyes missing hangs by its neck, the rope tied to a hook in the ceiling. Tom is over six feet, and it looks to Steve as though Tom's head almost touches the ceiling. Steve points at the bear and says, "What's this?"

"Nothing." Tom punches it, making it swing. "How old are you?"

"Thirteen."

"I thought so."

*

Vicki wishes Herbert would stop staring at her. After Tom and Steve go to the back of the trailer, Herbert comes over to her and takes her in his arms. She holds her cigarette behind him and hopes he lets go before the ash falls on the floor. "God, I love you," he says, and she pats his back with her free hand. When he lets go, he moves away from her a couple of feet and stares some more.

She's always been bothered by a certain look some men give her. They look desperate. Her ex-husband looked at her that way, even after their marriage fell apart. He'd give her the same desperate look he had given her when they were dating in high school, but he'd say, "You bitch. You goddamn bitch." Her brother-in-law Ed gave her that look, too.

"Quit gawkin' at me that way," she says to Herbert.

Then Steve comes back in. Lumbering in behind him is Tom, who was big and sweet when he was a baby; he weighed ten pounds at birth. He was always smiling and giggling. When he learned to talk, everything went down hill. He learned dirty words from hearing Vicki's ex-husband use them. By the time Tom turned eleven, he was as tall as Vicki. Now he looks like a man, a big slug of a man. It's almost as if he were some guy she picked up at a bar, brought home, and couldn't get rid of. And now, Jesus, she's got this other kid on her hands.

"Tom," Herbert says, "your mother tells me you just got your driver's license. Why don't you and Steve take a ride." He hands Tom the keys to the Buick. Vicki's '73 Dodge Swinger sits beside the trailer but hasn't run for a month.

*

Steve looks at his father and Vicki, their arms around each other's waist. They head back into the trailer before Tom finishes backing out and turning around.

Tom turns up the radio full blast and drives fast down back roads. He grins every time he makes a curve, the tires squealing. Steve laughs loud to show he's having a good time and isn't frightened. "You like baseball?" Steve yells above the music.

Tom shrugs and runs a stop sign.

They end up at a high school. "This your school?" Steve hollers.

Tom nods. Only four cars are in the parking lot. Tom presses down on the gas, then jerks the steering wheel, and they do a donut on the gravel. Then Tom slaps the gear shift into reverse, and like cars Steve's seen on "Demolition Derby," they attack a new Ford but stop about two inches before ramming it.

Tom jumps out, leaving his door open, and hops onto the hood of the Ford. He bounces on his toes a couple of times, then leaps, coming down on his heels. The hood buckles.

When he gets back in the car, he says, "Bitch gave me a F."

*

For supper that first night, they have boiled potatoes and a roast, a special supper Vicki has made. They leave the TV on while they eat, and when a commercial for Santo Gold comes on, Vicki runs over to see it. Then back at the table, she explains to Steve that she sells Santo Gold, which is prettier and cheaper than regular gold. She has her own business, she says, smiling. She sells necklaces and rings and bracelets at a flea market a quarter of a mile down the road. She has her own booth.

Steve has seen the outside of the flea market. It's a long white-washed building with dozens of bird baths and plaster animals out front.

*

The first couple of weeks at Vicki's, Steve doesn't do much except watch TV, take naps, and go to his new school. A few times he thinks about his mother and feels a little sorry for her but doesn't really miss her. His father keeps telling him he should call her, but he hasn't felt like it. Sometimes he looks at his baseball cards, which he hides because he's afraid Tom will do something to them. Tom said baseball cards were stupid.

Steve's father and Vicki go out every other night. Tom isn't around much either; when he is, he seldom talks to anyone. Herbert and Vicki always come home drunk, and Steve wakes up. He hears water running and the TV coming on loud and then going soft. Vicki calls Steve's father Ernie, and he calls her Betty. Steve has no idea why.

"Come on, Ernie, tell me. What he say? Why'd you wanta hit him?"

"No, Betty. Nope. I'm not gonna tell ya, Betty. Betty, you're beautiful. You know that, Betty?"

"Come on, Ernie. What'd he say? Why'd you try to start a fight?"

"Well, I'll tell you, Betty. He said, 'Your girl friend has a nice butt.' That's what he said, Betty. And I said, 'I don't cotton to no one talkin' 'bout Betty's butt.' "

"Cotton? Where the hell you get a word like that, Ernie? Is that the way hillbillies talk or somethin'?"

"The way bakers talk."

"That's the way rednecks talk. Or colored people. My daddy always called black people colored."

"What color?"

"Huh?"

"Nothin'."

"Anyway, Ernie, sweetie, that man was paying you a compliment. Your girlfriend has a great butt. What's wrong with sayin' that?"

These nights, Steve eventually dozes off to the murmurs of the TV. Or he hears them go into their bedroom, and his heart speeds up as he waits. He listens. And soon, through the thin wall, he hears them making love.

*

By the time Steve gets up each weekday morning, his father has been gone for three hours. Vicki usually stays in bed, and Tom catches early rides to school with friends. Steve eats cereal and watches cartoons. Sometimes he tries to do some homework he put off.

The junior high school he goes to now is in an old building with noisy steam-heat radiators. The textbooks are different. Some of the things the teachers talk about are things he learned long ago; other things are new and make no sense. Several of the teachers have custom-made paddles, made for them by students in the wood shop class at the high school.

One Monday morning a couple of weeks into November, instead of walking out to the highway to catch the school bus, Steve walks into the woods surrounding the mobile-home park. It's cold, but he waits until he's sure Vicki has gone to the flea market. Then he goes back to the trailer and makes a peanut-butter-and-jelly sandwich and watches MTV. Vicki has Showtime, but the movies on this morning are lousy: they're for kids.

The next day he goes to school. No one seems to have missed him, so on Wednesday he goes into the woods again and finds a trail that comes out onto the back lot of a King Kwik convenience store. He buys candy bars, and every day afterward when he decides not to go to school he goes to King Kwik for what he thinks of as "supplies." Walking through the woods, he pretends he's on a hiking trip or a military mission in a jungle.

One day around noon, while he's taking a nap, the trailer door opens. Steve panics. He tries to get out the back door, but Tom sees him. "Hey, kid, what you doing here?"

"I'm sick."

"Sick my ass."

Standing next to Tom is a skinny, thick-lipped boy with lank brown hair hanging in his eyes. The boy is holding a paper bag.

"We usually go to Roger's trailer," Tom says. "But his sister's home."

Tom and Roger sit down on the sofa and pass a bottle back and forth and stare at MTV. Finally, without saying anything, Tom passes it to Steve. Later, when Steve throws up, Tom says, "You'll get used to it."

"I've drunk it before," Steve says. "No lie."

*

Whenever he and Vicki don't go out, Herbert lets Tom borrow the Buick. When Steve starts going out with Tom,

Herbert tells Vicki he's glad the boys have become friends.

Tom, Roger, and Steve go to an abandoned farm house that sits far back from the highway down a gravel drive. In the crawl space under the house, they keep a supply of beer—hidden so that bums won't find it. At night they light candles, and they sit on the wood floors with blankets wrapped around themselves; there's no glass in the windows and the wind whistles through the rooms.

They drink beer and pee out the windows. Sometimes they talk about ways to get money. They think it would be easy to rob old people walking down a dark street.

Tom keeps a couple of porno magazines at the house, and he and Roger talk about girls. Tom says he's in love with a girl named Shirley. "She's a tease, but I love her. I really do, man. I'm gonna marry her."

Steve is sure he will. Tom says things as though he has no doubts, and Steve sees him as an adult, no different from Steve's father. But when Shirley comes with them to the farm one Sunday afternoon, Steve is disappointed. She's skinny, even skinnier than Roger, and her cheeks are hollow, as if she'd lost all her teeth. Her hair goes down past her shoulders, black for a couple of inches at the roots, almost white otherwise. She has thick, black eyebrows. *Brick shithouse*, Steve thinks.

She keeps saying she's cold, and Tom puts his arm around her and hugs her. While she drinks a beer, she looks at one of Tom's magazines, scrunching up her face and saying one girl is ugly, another fat. "All these girls are probably dead from AIDS by now," she says. She tosses the magazine across the room. "I'm cold."

"It's warmer in the car," Tom says, grinning at Roger.

Steve and Roger stay in the house. The wind whips through the windows. Roger wraps a blanket around himself and says, "I'd like to set this place on fire some day. You think it'd burn fast?"

"Why you wanta burn it down?"

Roger shrugs. "I don't know."

Steve belches. "We wouldn't have a house."

Roger shrugs again. Then they hear Shirley scream, and they jump up and run to the front porch. Shirley and Tom seem to be wrestling. They're beside the car on the grass, the driver's door open. Tom pulls back his arm three times as if to slap her, then finally does. Then he kisses her. Their breath makes fog that is whipped away by the wind. Steve doesn't know whether they're just fooling around or what.

Shirley laughs, then screams again, and Roger runs to them. He helps Tom hold her. Tom says something to him. The wind rushes through the high grass and the bare branches of the trees, and Tom's words are muffled. Roger runs to the barn, while Tom sits on Shirley's stomach and keeps her arms pinned.

Steve opens his mouth to say, "Be careful," but doesn't.

Roger has gotten rope, and Shirley screams and rolls her head and yells, "Stop it, you bastard!" while Roger ties her hands and feet. He has plenty of rope and runs a length of it from her neck to a tree. When he runs to the car and backs it toward Tom and Shirley, Steve thinks he's going to run over them. Steve feels dizzy and his stomach churns. He reaches out to grip the porch railing.

Roger stops just short of Shirley and Tom. Tom is grinning and stroking her hair. Roger ties another piece of rope to her ankles and the car's bumper.

When Tom gets off her, she lies still. He talks to her in a low voice. She lets out another scream when Tom and Roger get into the car. Steve steps inside the house and vomits in a corner. He hears Tom gunning the car's engine, and he keeps retching even after his stomach is empty.

Then he hears laughter, wild hoots carried by the wind. Shirley yells something, and Steve walks carefully to the porch. Shirley is standing between the car and the tree, the ropes gone. Tom hugs her, but she pulls away and slaps him.

*

One morning not long before Christmas, after going to King Kwik, Steve finds a powder-blue El Dorado parked beside Vicki's trailer. He goes back to the edge of the woods to a spot where he can wait and watch. It's freezing and the wind is up. He watches the wind whip laundry hanging behind one of the trailers. Bras flutter like strange birds. In a little while, a fat woman wearing earmuffs and a parka over a nightgown comes out of her trailer and takes the laundry down. Steve has seen her before but doesn't know her name. He doesn't know any of the neighbors' names.

He leans against a tree and eats a Hershey bar. A loose sheet of tin keeps slapping the side of a trailer. A bare-chested man opens the door of the trailer and leans out. He spits and says, "Damn!" The man's skin reminds Steve of marble.

Steve thinks about going back to King Kwik, but he doesn't have any more money. He doesn't pretend he's hiking in a woods or doing reconnaissance in a jungle, watching for bears or Viet Cong. He just wants to get inside the trailer—or somewhere, even school—out of the cold.

He thinks he might call his mother when he gets inside. If she doesn't cry or anything, talking to her might not be too bad.

A man comes out of Vicki's trailer. He looks old, maybe fifty. He has a lot of gray hair but his mustache is black, a stupid-looking little mustache like old movie stars used to have. He has on white shoes and a brown leather jacket. He's carrying a key chain that looks as though it's made out of Santo Gold. After he starts the El Dorado, Vicki comes out of the trailer and they drive away.

*

Steve wakes up. The room is pitch black. Tom is snoring softly. Steve hears someone in the kitchenette opening and closing the refrigerator door, someone clinking jars and rattling silverware, then running water.

A chair scrapes the floor. Silence. Then his father sighs

and says, "Vicki. Goddamn it. Goddamn it."

In a moment there's a low, wet moan. Steve feels himself drifting, falling back to sleep. "I'm just a baker," he hears. And he hears his father crying.

SAMSON

"Please tell me wherein
your great strength lies,
and how you might be bound,
that one could subdue you."

ONE

Samson hears the screen door squeak, opens his eyes, and is blinded by the Oklahoma sun. He has been lying in the sun like a white whale beached on the patch of grass in front of his and Lou Ann's mobile home, wondering why God lets a son of a bitch like him live. He lifts his head and distressfully notes (not for the first time) that he can't see his feet for his belly; he remembers when he looked like Mr. America. "Lou, honey." A shadow falls over him. He begins to turn his head, and this is when it suddenly rains a gallon of Coca-Cola Lou Ann has poured from bottles into a tin bucket she usually fills with hot water and Spic 'n Span.

"Oh, honey, I deserve it. I know I do." The screen door slams. The lock clicks. Samson is standing now, wiping his face with the red beach towel he was lying on. "Now, honey, let me in there. I gotta wash this stuff off. Good God, honey," and he laughs, "the red ants will probably attack me and eat me alive."

For a minute the space behind the screen is gray like early morning, then fills with the colors of Lou Ann. She is six feet three inches tall and weighs a hundred and ninety pounds: a great big, pink beautiful woman with orange hair and green eyes who used to call herself Lola, The Goddess of Sweet Sin and wrestle other big women. She is wearing lime green shorts that are tight and bulge with her thighs. And a red and white striped blouse about to burst with her breasts. "I hope them ants start with your pecker."

"Honey, watch what you say now. The neighbors will hear you. And Tina Lee, too. Where is Tina Lee? Did she hear you say that word?"

"She's sleepin'. She can't hear and she's too little to understand anyway. I hope they chew up your balls and spit 'em out."

"Honey." Samson winces and squeezes his knees together. He looks down at the ground. No ants yet.

He looks around at the mobile homes nearby. In the one next to theirs, an old rusty white one with fake shutters and a fake gable, lives the nosiest and ugliest woman Samson has ever known, uglier than even poor Jean Marie, his twin sister, who lives with his mama and will never get married, no way. The neighbor is a pile of lumps, two lumps for calves, two for thighs, a huge undulating one for a butt, another lump for a torso, and disproportionately small ones for breasts and a head. Every time he steps outside, Samson sees her face at one of her windows, her fat loose lips nearly pressed against the glass. Her hair is mousy gray, long and straight like a young girl's, but she must be older than he is, forty-three. He imagines that this hideous woman, who surely has never had a man, must be craving him, and when he has this thought, blurry images appear in his mind, and he shudders the way he does when The Mean Mongolian puts a Boston Crableg hold on him and he's supposed to be in pain that no one in the arena or watching at home can imagine.

"I don't know why you have to leave *tonight*," Lou Ann says.

"I told you, honey, I'm sorry, but I got to be in Dallas in the morning to see that promoter Hoffman. It's real important business."

"Can't you change the time?"

"Lou, you're bein' unreasonable now. This is the way you was with Tina Lee, too." He looks at the section of the door behind which Lou Ann's belly is hidden, where a new baby is growing. He imagines her belly gently swelling out from her ribs.

Just yesterday they found out. Samson sat in the waiting room of the OB's office, across from the cute little nurse, nut brown from the sun. When she got up from behind her desk and turned her back to slip a file into a cabinet, he tried to picture her in one of those two-piece bathing suits.

He wasn't sure whether she kept smiling at him because she had a good idea he was going to be a daddy again—everybody likes soon-to-be daddies, as if they must be naturally nice people if God would give them a little baby—or whether she got wet between the thighs looking at such a big and powerful man, a TV celebrity, a professional athlete—well, wrestler—but, God, she was young enough to be his daughter; flirting would be a sin, especially under the circumstances, with his big beautiful wife he loved so much getting checked to see whether her being sick and bitchy was because she was pregnant. The funny thing about that little nurse, only about five feet tall with dark hair long down her back, was that she looked a lot like Candy, the real reason he had to be in Dallas in the morning.

"Honey, let me in now." Some flies are gathering on his head and shoulders. Slapping at them, he walks up the three wooden steps and stands with his nose less than an inch from the screen. "Please, honey."

Finally, she breaks down, flips up the lock latch and lets him in, but she immediately hurries down the hall and into their bedroom, shutting and locking the door behind her. Just like a goddamn child, Samson thinks. Crazy when she's pregnant. And for a moment he holds his breath as he glares at the closed bedroom door, before he goes into the bathroom, a tiny pink room that is almost like a closet for Samson, who weighs two hundred and eighty-eight pounds. He pulls down his bathing trunks and sees no difference between the color of his hips and the rest of him. A white fish belly of a body covered with swirls of black hair. It seems to Samson that his shoulders get shaggier as he loses the hair on his head. Seeing himself in the bathroom mirror prompts him to reach into the medicine cabinet for a green bottle of clear liquid he saw advertised in the back of *Baseball* magazine. The label says that extreme caution must be taken in the use of the "tonic" because it promotes the growth of hair on *any* surface it touches.

He imagines clumps of hair on the end of his nose, on his palms, and because he got the stuff on his fingers then peed, on the end of his pecker. He doesn't now because he would only wash it off in the shower, but when he does use it, he carefully pours a small amount on a pad of cloth and dabs it gingerly on the top of his skull. "This stuff is shit," he's been mumbling to himself as the weeks have passed and nothing grows, but he always washes his hands thoroughly.

A minute or two after he steps into the shower, Lou Ann pulls back the shower curtain, startling him. She giggles at his woman-like gasp. Who did he expect? For a second, a maniac. Like in *Psycho.* Janet Leigh. Nice tits, Janet Leigh. You could almost see them all in that shower scene. But they weren't as nice as Lou Ann's.

Lou Ann is naked. Rosy pink, not white like him, nice

and pink with a big triangle of orange pubic hair, the bushiest one he's ever seen. As she steps into the shower, he lifts his arms to take her in, and she stoops, as if a shy child, snuggling her face in his graying chest hair. He kisses the top of her skull and pats her soft, fleshy back with one hand, the fingers of the other pressing into a cheek of her broad butt. When she stands straight, they are eye to eye, hers green, his blue like a swimming pool with a painted bottom. The water beats down on them. They kiss. He leans her against the back wall of the stall, and he pictures the trailer leaning with their weight and motion, pictures it toppling over onto its side, but he wouldn't care. Kissing her neck. Fondling one of her breasts, which hang heavy, low as her belly button. They are incredible.

When he turns off the water, they hear Tina Lee crying.

In the dining area he sits across from Tina Lee in her high chair, feeding her apple sauce and creamed spinach that looks like something somebody threw up, while by the stove Lou Ann in a pink robe works at fixing supper. She's humming a ballad she heard on "American Bandstand." A good voice. She can be so sweet when she's not bitchy.

"We're gonna need more room, Sam, now that another baby's comin'."

"Maybe we can get a trailer with three bedrooms." He remembers seeing one that had mirrors all along a wall of the biggest bedroom and red wallpaper with silver cupids all over it. That would be nice. But then he thinks that that kind of decor might not be such a good idea; it might be a bad influence on his children when they got older. Teenagers. Jesus, teenagers are crazy. Look at "American Bandstand." Look at his boy Daryl Junior, sullen and lazy and crazy about rock 'n' roll.

Still nice, though—mirrors all along the wall. But in ten years, 1972, will he want to look at himself? (Jesus, 1972, people will be driving those bubble-top cars.) Lou Ann is only twenty-eight; she'll be okay unless she lets herself go, but he will be fifty-three, and the way his belly is getting out of control, he has already seen the last of his dick—need a mirror—although he keeps swearing to himself he'll go on a diet. Mr. America he used to look like. Mr. Universe. Fifty-inch chest, twenty-inch arms, thirty-two-inch waist.

"I was thinkin'," Lou Ann says, her back to him, "we could maybe buy a house. We should have plenty saved, the way you wrestle five or six nights a week. I do wish you'd let me know more about our money." She turns to face him. "I don't mean to be morbid or nothin', but what if you was to die? I wouldn't know nothin'."

She might find out plenty.

Death might be good. A way out. A flood of images fills his head. Bank figures. Accounts here in Oklahoma City, also in Dallas and Houston. Faces: Candy; Dana Diane; Daryl Junior; Earl; Benny Bob; Buddy Hoffman, the prick; Mama; Jean Marie.

Oh, Lord, he is a crazy son of a bitch, a bigamist. And he's supporting Candy, good as married to her but without the piece of paper, which she is getting itchy for. "What if I got pregnant?" Candy keeps saying. Oh, Lord, not that. Three boys with Dana Diane. Two babies now with Lou Ann. Crazy. Mama would die of shame if she knew. Jean Marie would probably be happy as hell: she hates him.

Samson is quiet throughout supper. Lou Ann asks if something is wrong. No. What could be?

Afterward, Tina Lee is asleep in her crib back in her cubbyhole of a room. Lou Ann sits on the sofa watching the big RCA TV that cost Samson a week's worth of wrestling matches. He bought it the same day he signed the lease on the little brick house in Dallas where he and Candy live. The old lady who owned the house asked him whether he and his daughter—Jesus, his daughter—were from Dallas. Candy burst out laughing, loud and shrill, the only way she ever laughs. But she didn't say a word and even stifled herself when Samson said, "My daughter and me are from Oklahoma." So all on the same day, he signed the lease, kissed Candy good-bye, drove to Oklahoma City, went to a TV store and bought the RCA TV in a maple cabinet and presented it to Lou Ann as a surprise, as a way of saying he was sorry for something Lou Ann knew nothing about.

Lou Ann is watching "The Dick Van Dyke Show" and eating Sun-Kist raisins. Samson is at the table where they eat their meals. Scattered on it now are the plastic pieces of a model car. Samson likes to build models, to pour out onto a table the jumbled contents of a box, take that mess and make something nice: no glue showing, the rough edges filed down. Back in his and Lou Ann's bedroom he has put up shelves on which there sit cars and airplanes and ships: '36 Cord, '32 Cadillac, '48 Dodge, '38 Chevy, *The Spirit of St. Louis*, the *Bismarck*.

The one he's working on now is a '25 T-Model Ford. He had a real one in 1936 when he was seventeen (looked like Mr. Universe), and he drove it all the way up to Wisconsin to join the circus.

In a little while he gets ready to leave for Dallas, having stayed as late as he can. As he changes clothes he sees the patches of pink sunburn that have started to hurt. He doesn't understand why the burn is uneven. There is a stripe of painful pink down the middle of his sloping belly. There are also pink stripes on his arms and legs. His nose looks like a cherry. He wanted some color for his Texas Cage Death Match in two days; he will wear an outfit showing a lot of flesh. He looks, he thinks, like a barber's pole.

He puts his suitcase in the car, then comes back into the trailer to kiss Tina Lee and Lou Ann one more time. Outside, it's dark, the lightning bugs thick. Because he weighs two hundred and eighty-eight pounds, he figures his heart has to be pretty big. And as he holds up Tina Lee, rubbing his sore nose against hers, he feels that whole big heart swell with love. She has a clump of orange hair on the top of her head but is still bald for the most part. She has green eyes and a little rabbit nose like Lou Ann's. Where are his genes? Maybe in the weak chin, the long earlobes. She weighs over seventeen pounds now, but when she was born she weighed only six. Lou Ann swelled up to a radiant two hundred and twenty-six pounds—he'd never seen such breasts in his life; she could have been in a circus with those things—then that tiny kitten had slipped out.

She giggles at the nose rubbing. Then for no reason he can see, the little mouth stretches big and round, and a second later an ear-piercing wail erupts from it. Samson hugs her and rocks her and pats her and looks to Lou Ann for an explanation, for help.

"She knows her daddy's leavin' her again."

Amazed by what Lou Ann has said, amazed by the powers of this little child, he looks at Tina Lee's scarlet face, holding her at arms' length now and squinting his eyes at her as if to get her in focus. He looks at Lou Ann again. Something sickening is happening in his heart.

"She's gonna miss her daddy."

It is as if a balloon full of blood has suddenly risen to his head and burst. He sees red. He drapes Tina Lee over his huge forearm, and his big paw starts stinging her bottom like a swarm of bees. The trailer fills with the cries and the smacks. He is moaning, "Shut up, shut up."

Lou Ann grabs his arm and tries to hold it back. "Sam, are you crazy? You're just makin' it worse." Her big breasts and the roll around her middle jiggle; her hair, piled up on top of her head and pinned in place, unravels and falls in her face splotched pink and red.

When he stops, he realizes he is sweating like the colored boys he sometimes wrestles, and everything he sees—Tina Lee, Lou Ann, the RCA TV—is blurred, and there are little explosions of light everywhere, stars popping and fading. The baby is screaming. Lou Ann is yelling nasty things. Bitchy. Bitchy when she is and is not pregnant. He loves her anyway. She disappears for a moment with Tina Lee. The stars are still exploding. Jesus, what is the matter with him? He rubs his eyes, wants to cry. She returns without Tina Lee and attacks him with a heavy bronze ashtray she grasps easily in her big hand, putting welts on his forehead and the top of his skull before he can get out the door.

He storms out—tears the screen door off one of its hinges, thinks about turning the trailer over onto its side. But he just stands there in the dark, glaring at the yellow trailer. Mosquitoes buzz around the light above the door, which suddenly goes out.

The thumping of his heart fills his head. From somewhere, barely piercing the racket in his brain, come the words, "Oh, God, the guilt." Finally, he runs up to the trailer, kicks a dent in its side, then flees.

In his brand new 1962 Cadillac Eldorado he cuts through the night at eighty-five miles an hour, whipping past slower cars and those giant trucks that usually scare him. He drives a hundred miles before he remembers to put his glasses on, which he needs since he's become nearsighted in the last couple of years. He plays with the electric windows, letting air rush in, then cutting it off. The radio blares: Hank Williams, Johnny Cash, Conway Twitty, Loretta Lynn. . . .

After another hour or so, he lifts his glasses and squeezes the bridge of his nose between thumb and forefinger, and the tears pour down. The white Cadillac weaves. He grips the steering wheel with both hands. His foot eases up on the accelerator. He turns down the hillbilly on the radio.

Sweet Lou Ann.

Good idea: steer into the path of one of those trucks. Solve all his problems in this world. A big crash, then that long drop to Hell. Land in burning embers. Brimstone.

But he would miss Lou Ann. He remembers the first time he saw her. In Stillwater, Oklahoma, in the high school gym, in 1959. He was the star of the evening, scheduled to wrestle The Kansas Killer as the main event after the ladies had their cat fight. The bleachers were half empty. Mean-looking red-faced cowboys and young boys chewing tobacco. Lou Ann was decked out in what looked like a majorette's costume, tight and silver, her long meaty thighs all out there to see. Her opponent was a three-hundred pound woman who called herself Little Lil, blood-red fingernails to go with her blubber. She sat on the head of Lola, The Goddess of Sweet Sin, and tortured her.

Lou Ann approached him after his match. She was all cleaned up, her luscious orange hair shiny in the gym lights, her high heels making her taller than he was, her fingers glittering with gold and glass. Never in his life had he heard of a decent woman asking a man to have a drink with her. Never had he cheated on Dana Diane; she was the mama of his boys and, besides, he knew what it was like to be cheated on.

"I was married once when I was in the circus," he told Lou Ann, her incredible breasts actually *lying* on the table they sat at in a bar full of cowboys. "I was with a circus from 1936 till 1940." Her green eyes sparkled and she kept a little grin on her face. "I was the strong man. I bent iron bars, juggled cannon balls, lifted five hundred pounds with my teeth. It was all real, too. Nothin' phony. I got dentures now, I got to tell you. Anyway, my marriage didn't last long, just a couple months."

"Was your wife in the circus?" She sipped her beer. She had told him she was a city girl from Tulsa and liked wrestling a lot better than waitressing.

"She did tricks with lions."

"What she look like? Was she pretty?"

"She was okay."

"Those circus girls are always pretty doll-like things. Little."

"I like big women myself," he blurted out. "She was a phony blonde."

"I guess you'd know," she said coyly.

He felt himself blush. "That ain't what I meant."

She kept grinning. "So what happened to her?"

"I caught her with a clown."

Lou Ann burst out laughing. "I'm sorry, sugar. What you do?" Then she laughed some more.

Samson had broken six of the clown's ribs and his pretty young wife's nose, but he said, "I just yelled some."

"That's sad." Then she hooted a couple of more times. "I'm sorry, Sam, but I keep seein' some clown with blue hair and a big red nose and all."

Samson started to get mad.

But then Lou Ann said, "She must of been a fool."

"Why's that?"

She acted shy now. "You're a handsome man. And you seem real nice."

As Samson remembers this, he can almost believe she meant it. Three years ago he was thirty-five pounds lighter and had a lot more hair.

TWO

Early in the Texas morning the tires of his Eldorado crunch the gravel of Candy's driveway. The house is small and built out of ugly red bricks and is surrounded by houses just like it. The yard is bare of shrubs and trees and flowers. The weedy grass has turned brown. Every time he drives up to this place, he thinks he should get Candy something nicer, but money's a problem. The Cadillac, which he loves—if it were a woman, he has told Candy, the sight of it would make him hard—is a necessity, he rationalizes, although he would be better off with a cheap Ford and could then maybe afford to get Candy a nicer place and Dana Diane a dishwasher and Lou Ann a house instead of a trailer. The Cadillac is part of an image, though—an image that Lou Ann married, that Candy shacked up with, and that Dana Diane has grown used to in recent years.

The porch light is on, yellow, and he thinks about the

light on Lou Ann's trailer going out. Candy's door is unlocked for any rapist who wants to walk in or any son of a bitch fat phony who loves and is mean to too many women.

The living room is four white walls. Not much. A couple of brown rugs on the linoleum floor. Mostly junky furniture: a dark-green tweed sofa, a rocking chair with a broken slat, a scarred up coffee table, a TV on a rusty metal stand. These are all things Candy had in a tiny apartment in a bad section of town thick with Mexicans and Negroes.

Candy thinks that Samson has lived in motel rooms all his adult life and has paid most of his income to a greedy government and given the rest to needy relations; so she doesn't ask for much and, anyway, thinks the little house is nice. Still, Samson has gotten her a few things. One stands in a corner of the living room, looking as out of place as his Cadillac would in a junk yard: a thousand-dollar grandfather's clock.

Despite its shabbiness, the living room is clean. Candy is trying to demonstrate her housekeeping skills, showing that she will make a good wife. She's been cooking, too. In the kitchen is an apple pie, from which Samson scoops out a hunk with his big paw. He eats standing next to the new dishwasher.

In the bedroom, on the wall over the new brass bed is a big iron crucifix. There are dabs of red paint on Jesus' hands and feet. It must weigh fifteen pounds, and Samson is afraid it will fall one night. It could kill him. Why Candy wants that dangerous Jesus to watch them fornicate he'll never understand. She's a Catholic; his mama warned him about Catholics.

The chest of drawers and the nightstand are white, little-girl pieces of furniture, marked up and old, bought by Candy at a used-furniture store after she left home—a shack, she has told him, on a dried-up piece of what was supposed to be a farm in southwestern Texas.

Moonlight slants though the window, falling on Candy,

making her dark skin luminescent. She is spread out on her back in the heat, naked, her mouth open slightly and snoring softly. Samson takes off all his clothes and eases into bed, not wanting to wake her, this prize he cannot believe he has won. Then in his exhaustion, half asleep, he wonders what she does with her time. She has no job—she used to be a waitress. She can't watch TV all day, can she? Make pies? Dust? Mop? And maybe screw skinny-assed Mexicans right here in his brass bed? No. He wants to trust her. He tries. He has no reason not to. Turning, he gently pats her arm, kisses a nipple.

But how can he believe that she would be true to a fat old man like him? She is barely twenty and has fine black hair like an Indian's, straight and shimmering all the way down to her tail bone. Her body is like a Las Vegas show girl's— the roundest, smoothest bottom he has ever seen.

She rolls onto her side and opens her eyes, black, and without a word, starts loving him. Slick and shiny with sweat, she moves and groans on top of him, clutching his hairy shoulders. Jesus, he swears to himself as he always does in these moments. Isn't this what men live for? She leans her head down and brushes his belly with her hair. Faster and faster she rides him, making husky sounds that remind him of when Dana Diane was in labor.

Now Candy presses her face against his neck and her noises become higher pitched, even shrill. Jesus, he will never go to the others again, give up wrestling, hide out, move to Utah—where the Mormons are—and live on a mountain where he will screw the rest of his life away. His sunburn hurts but the hell with that.

Then calm. Fatigue. Sleep.

He dreams that Dana Diane is laid out in a coffin. In real life, she is skinny, frail as a granny. In the dream, the coffin is only about three inches wide but wide enough for her yellow corpse. Samson keeps asking everybody—his three boys, his mama, even Candy and Lou Ann—what happened, and they tell him it was her heart, how it kept shrinking with the rest of her. He wakes up crying.

Candy awakes, too, and presses herself against him, hurting his sunburn, and kisses his tears, sleepily saying, "What's wrong, you big ole thing? Is a monster gonna get ya?"

When he gets out of bed in the afternoon, Candy makes him fried eggs and waffles while he showers and shaves. In this medicine cabinet, too, there is a bottle of the stuff that is supposed to grow hair on an apple.

The hair on top of his head is thinner than ever, while the long hair on the sides and back hang limp to his shoulders, graying. Maybe, he thinks, he'll color it platinum or white, the color of the wig he wears when he wrestles as Bible Bob. His hair has always been long because of his Samson bit, in younger days hanging in his eyes; it is shorn now not by a beautiful Delilah, he thinks—he always pictures Hedy LaMar—but by that old bitch Age.

And it isn't just his hair that bothers him; it is his whole face. It is scarred from teenage acne and has gotten puffy-looking. When he locks the bathroom door and removes his dentures to clean them, he becomes an old, old man.

Wearing the white robe Candy gave him last Christmas—Lord, was that a mess, trying to spend some Christmas with each woman—he ambles into the kitchen, depressed; and standing by the table, watching Candy, who's wearing tight denim shorts and a red halter, work at the stove, he says, "I don't know why you love a fat old man like me."

She puts down her spatula, turns, hugs him, and steps back to the stove, and says, "You're bein' silly when you say such things."

He sits down, not knowing what else to say, listens to the popping grease. Then, "I'm gonna buy you a new stove. You go pick one out. Anything you want."

"General Electric?"

"Hell, you can get a Cadillac stove if you want."

She sets his food before him. "Hear what President Kennedy did?"

This interest in politics is strange. She's a prize, but she's also a dumb country girl and a child. Of course the answer is that she has no real interest in politics, only in a pretty-boy dream man she probably thinks about when fat old men are on her. "Too bad you ain't old enough to vote," anger and hurt rising from his heart, "but I bet you'd like to lay Kennedy, wouldn't you?"

"Sometimes you're crazy, Sammy."

"Man's younger than me and he's the goddamned president."

"He just looks younger. He's two years older."

Samson glares. "Thanks."

"Oh, Sammy!"

"You know a lot about him."

"Sammy." She stands with her hands on her hips and smiles down at him. "He ain't never been a world champion at nothin'," she says.

"Shiiit," Samson drawls.

"Let's talk about somethin' else." She sits down across from him. He looks at her deep cleavage. They're not big enough to have to lie on the table like Lou Ann's, but there's plenty. Sweet things. She is truly a prize. "Let's talk about gettin' married."

He was feeling horny for a minute, but this cools him off. "Now, hon, I don't know."

"Oh, come on, Sammy. Let's pick a day."

"I told you, honey, I don't know. I mean not now. Me on the road all the time." He stuffs a waffle in his mouth and chews.

"What if I got pregnant?"

He chews for a long time. She waits. "You won't," he says. "I'm too old to get girls knocked up." He laughs, thinks of Lou Ann, takes another big bite of waffle and almost chokes.

"President Kennedy. . . . Well, never mind."

She gets up and goes into the living room and turns on a

soap opera. A few minutes later, he asks her to get him a Coke, and she does and even kisses his cheek. Not like Lou Ann. Candy doesn't sulk much or bitch or slam doors. More grown up in some ways. Or maybe she's just waiting to get the ring, then *bam!*

He has an hour and a half before he has to go see Buddy Hoffman. Candy is interested in her soap opera, so he goes to the hall closet, gets out a box, and pours the plastic contents onto the kitchen table. He's working on a '32 Packard.

Samson would love to piss on Buddy Hoffman's head. Whenever he walks into Hoffman's office, which in the summer is a hundred degrees with one little fan on the desk blowing in Hoffman's fat acne-scarred face (Oh, God, he doesn't look like that, too, does he? Samson worries; he has the horrible feeling that he and Hoffman are almost twins), Samson's stomach churns hate, pukes that hate up into his head, making his head throb painfully.

Today, when Samson enters the office, Hoffman is reading a newspaper and smoking a Camel. He rises from his chair and offers a hand dirty with sweat and ink. Samson holds his breath as if Hoffman stinks and makes the handshake short. To squeeze his hand and crush it would be a delight.

"What you want to see me about?"

"Sit, Sam, sit."

Giving orders to him like he's a dog.

"How would you like to wrestle some bouts in Mexico?" In the past four years Hoffman has become the biggest promoter of Southwest World Championship Wrestling. He decides who wrestles when and where and for how much. How he got so much control Samson doesn't know.

"Wouldn't."

Hoffman smiles big. "Let me explain."

"Would it pay more?"

"I can't say yet."

"I got a family I don't see enough as is."

Hoffman leans forward and places his palms flat on top of the metal desk. "Hear me out, Daryl," he says, using Samson's real name.

Hoffman is about forty-five, Samson figures. A fat man, bald on top, balder than he is by far. Hoffman was a screen-writer and actor in Hollywood for twenty years, probably never doing anything any good: at least Samson never heard of him. But two things Samson has to hand the man: he has good taste in cars—a sky-blue Cadillac Eldorado—and women—a young blonde with tits like melons. When Hoffman attends matches, which is seldom, she is always on his arm.

"We're expanding into Mexico, see, or trying to. We'll hold matches in a lot of the border towns. The spics and tourists down there love wrestling and we can do a lot of things there we can't here."

"Do things?"

"Stuff in the ring."

"Like what?"

"I'll explain later."

What can the bastard mean? They already do just about everything there is to do in the way of physical torture and abuse. Of course, it's all fake. Maybe he means it won't be fake down there. Real blood. Real broken bones. Backs. This son of a bitch wouldn't care as long as he gets his money. (Samson has heard that regardless of the shit-hole office Hoffman is rich and lives in a hundred-thousand-dollar house.) Or maybe there'd be something having to do with sex? Have naked lady wrestlers? Maybe men, too? Something having to do with animals?

"I ain't doin' no crap in Mexico."

"Hey, it'll be fun, Daryl. Maybe we can work something out with the money, a good deal, you being a vet after all— of how many years?"

"Seventeen."

"Right. And a former world champ."

"More money, you say?"

"Sure."

"Now what exactly we gonna do down there?"

"Well, I want you to be The Masked Demon exclusively."

"I'd never be Samson?"

"No."

"No Bible Bob?"

"No. But the tourists and the spics will love The De-mon."

"The usual act?"

"We'll add some things."

"Like what?"

"Well, I don't want to go into it now. I have to check into the legal ends of a few things yet. I don't want to explain until I know exactly what we can do."

Samson's head is leaned to one side. He squints his eyes. "You want me to screw pigs or somethin'?"

Hoffman laughs. "Now, Daryl, let's just drop it for now. I already talked to Berry Brown by the way. And The Arab and Jake The Snake and Handsome Harry, and they're all willing to wrestle down there."

"Those guys all probably screw pigs for a hobby. Just tell me what I'd have to do."

"Be The Demon."

"What else?"

"Nothing. Nothing much." The son of a bitch keeps smiling. One hand is lying on the top of the other now. He looks prim and proper sitting there that way with his lips pursed and wearing a white shirt and a tie, except for the giant sweat stains under his arms.

"I don't trust you."

"Daryl, you're paranoid. Hey, you all set for tonight? I have to admit the Dallas fans go for Bible Bob. In Mexico he'd flop. But here he's great."

"I ain't wrestlin' in Mexico. I got a family I need to spend time with."

"How is the family?"

"They're good."

"They're in Oklahoma City?"

"Yeah." Samson blinks fast three times. And his heart takes off like a race horse out of a chute. He stares at Hoffman. He has always told Hoffman his wife and kids are in Houston. Does the son of a bitch know something?

"I'd like to meet the good woman some time when I'm down there."

Did he emphasize the word "Down"? He *knows*, Samson thinks. Oh, Lord, the son of a bitch knows.

"Tell you what, Daryl. The Mexican thing. No rush. Give me a call in a day or two and we'll talk some more."

Hoffman gets up and walks to the door with Samson. He pats Samson's sweat-soaked back.

Samson doesn't say a word. He just leaves.

Tonight Candy puts on a sequined body suit and a velour cowboy hat, and she and Samson go together to the arena, where she sits in the same front-row seat she had fourteen months ago when Samson asked Mr. Wonderful, a sun-burnished pretty boy, to throw him out of the ring and at her feet, so he could introduce himself.

He had noticed her for a couple of months, cheering him, Bible Bob, on with her shrill country yells, jumping to her feet every few seconds, waving a pretty little fist with pink painted nails and twitching her shapely bottom in such a way that the cowboys behind her whistled for *her*, the hell with the guys in the ring. He had started waving and nodding and smiling at her. In his dimly lit hotel room, green paint peeling in the corners of the ceiling, he would lie on the bed and think of her, picturing her white teeth and pink tongue, her breasts, her nipples hard.

After the Mr. Wonderful match, he had a late supper with her and listened to her talk about how she loved the excitement of professional wrestling; about her daddy she had loved so much, who shriveled up and dried out like his farm; about her nasty mama who tortured her poor daddy with stories of how her great beauty could have caught her a rich husband instead of a failure; about her job as a waitress and how she had never known how rude people could be. He told her he had been married once, twenty years ago to a phony blonde who did tricks with lions and clowns.

Only after he'd taken her out three months (to movies, fancy restaurants, nightclubs) and bought her hundreds of flowers and fifty or sixty pounds of expensive candy did she go to bed with him. And this fact gave him comfort, assured him she was no whore; that is, if she wasn't playing him for a fat old fool, trying to get out of him as many free meals and flowers as she could, while when he wasn't around she laid every cowboy in the city. For those three months, she'd kiss him, nice and wet, but she kept her knees together. When she finally gave in (and he was always trying), she said it was because she loved him: he was a big sweet old thing, mature, funny, interesting, and wise. And he loved her, too, he blubbered, and meant it. He wept, his head buried between her naked breasts, a dream come true.

Tonight Candy screams for Bible Bob to mutilate that no good Russian, Igor Tolstoy, whose red wrestling suit bears on the front and back the Soviet hammer and sickle.

Before the bout Bible Bob, as friendly and as happy as could be, explained to the weasel-faced little cologne-stinking TV announcer that his mission in life was to kick butt for God.

"Tell us, Bible Bob, how will you fend off Igor Tolstoy, The Mad Russian's, nefarious paralyzer hold?"

With a big friendly smile Bible Bob, wearing a white wrestling suit with a white cape that helped hide his fat, looked straight into the camera: "All I can say is that Jesus is in my corner. I hope to get my soul saver hold on this Russian and transmit to him some of the love I have. I love everybody 'cause I got Jesus in my heart. And Jesus *is* love."

During the bout, as he and Igor grapple and punch and poke and kick, Samson can occasionally glance at his prize and the people behind her: cowboys; fat slum women and their retarded-looking kids; angry frail men who work in warehouses or factories; winos dragged in off the streets for televised bouts so the arena is full. They all seem to think it is real. Candy, too.

Toward the end of the match, Igor has Bible Bob against the ropes, stamping his foot on the canvas to make a lot of noise as he throws a rapid succession of punches, and the fans are furious. A chant of "Kill the commie" starts up. Bible Bob groans, calls for Jesus (an old woman in the audience screeches, "Please, sweet Jesus, help the man!"), raises his right arm, spreads his fingers, and jerks his head to the side with each blow, Igor's knuckles wheezing past his chin an inch away. It is strange how his fingers tingle when he splays them like that and calls to God. It is spooky and wonderful.

Eventually, Bible Bob breaks free, picks Igor up, and does a back breaker across his knee. Then while Igor, now a cowardly instead of a mad Russian, is on his knees, shaking his head and pleading with raised arms for mercy, Bible Bob places his hand on Igor's forehead and shouts, "Out all demons! Love! Love!"

Igor faints, topples over backwards, and remains unconscious long enough to be counted out; then after regaining consciousness, he follows Bob around the ring, Bob waving and strutting, Igor crawling on his knees and shouting in an accent that is a mixture of Mississippi redneck and TV Russian, "Oh, thank you! I seen the light, comrade!"

In bed with Candy at one-thirty in the morning, Samson can't sleep. For one thing his back aches—more because of Candy than Igor. She is softly snoring now and drooling a little from the side of her mouth. He pats her head and his heart swells. Does Hoffman know about her, too? If he knows about Lou Ann, he probably does. But does he really know anything? If he does, how did he find out? Private eyes? Guys with little cameras and snub-nosed revolvers. He eases out of bed and goes to the kitchen table where the unfinished Packard sits. He has been sloppy with it; glue bubbles out of the seams. He dials Hoffman's number, and after it rings a dozen times, a woman answers. "Yeah?" Samson can see the platinum hair, the big tits.

"Can I speak to Hoffman?"

She doesn't say anything; then Hoffman is on the line. "Who is this?"

"It's Sam."

"Daryl? Where are you?"

"I wanta talk to you 'bout Mexico."

"I was about to give you hell, but since it's you—it's one of my star wrestlers," he says to his wife. Samson hears her laugh. "You've been thinking about Mexico, huh? I tell you, it's going to be great. The Demon will be a big hit with the spics and all the tourists bombed on tequila."

"I wanta know," Samson whispers, "more about it."

"We'll work something out with the money. Maybe we can even cut a match or two from your usual circuit so you won't be away from your family so much."

"What do you know, Hoffman?" he says quickly, unable to hold the question back.

"About what?"

"You know what I mean."

"I do?"

"Yeah."

"Hey, you know, it really is late." Then Samson hears the woman say, "Tell the asshole to fuck off."

"Hoffman, tell me."

"Listen, I don't know what the hell you're talking about."

It is like taking a drink of cold water when he is really thirsty after a long match or after sucking the sauce off Dana Diane's pork chops or after a long sweaty love session with Candy. Hoffman knows nothing. He's just a butterball going bald faster than Samson is. Nothing.

"Listen, Hoffman, I'm sorry I woke you up or whatever I did. I ain't wrestlin' in Mexico, though. That's what I wanted to tell you."

There is silence, then the tolling of the grandfather's clock in the living room.

"Listen, Daryl," Hoffman says sweetly, "you think some more about it. I know you're a family man, but Houston isn't so far from some of those border towns. It is Houston where your family is, isn't it? It's not like they were in Oklahoma or somewhere else."

Samson hangs up the phone without another word.

He paces in the dark little kitchen, trembling. Then wanting to be near Candy, he goes back to bed. He can see all the love going out of his life—Lou Ann, Candy, Dana Diane all falling from him into some black hole. Mama, too—ashamed to call him her son. And maybe he deserves whatever he gets. Hoffman isn't the only son of a bitch. He thinks about spanking Tina Lee last night, spanking her because he hated himself. Now did that make any goddamn sense?

At Lou Ann's, he thinks, he is always telling her to shut that child up or to clean that dirty child up or to make that kid eat her food so she won't grow up lacking brain cells and be a retarded person like he thinks her mother is sometimes.

God, he is a bastard. God, little Tina Lee is the sweetest thing, all soft and round and pretty and pink, just like her mama, who is going to be a mama again.

He weeps and eases up out of bed to go into the bathroom where he sits on the toilet with the lid down. Suddenly, being in bed with Candy was making him feel worse about himself, more and more like a son of a bitch who didn't deserve to live and have three fine women and four beautiful children, to have so much love, so much love that his heart can barely hold it all. That is why he cannot give up any of his families: he loves them all, although loving them all is wrong and makes him sick in his soul. How, *how*, with so much love can he be such a son of a bitch?

Because he likes to think that there is some kind of order in the world, that chaos can be fit together in a certain way so everything will make sense, Samson wonders if his being a son of a bitch has anything to do with being a bad guy wrestler most of the time these days. He hates being a bad guy, despite the fact he's pretty good at it (sometimes he even brags to Dana Diane about how he can really rile up the fans).

He's Bible Bob only in Dallas. In most cities he's The Masked Demon, Hoffman's idea. As The Masked Demon, Samson wears a red mask over his whole head, narrow slits bordered in black for his eyes, nose, and mouth. And a red wrestling suit with long sleeves and pants legs and with a long pointed tail, which he wraps around his opponents' necks and sometimes trips over. In the TV interviews he grabs the microphone from the announcer and chants, "I love evil, I love blood, I love death!" When the announcer tries to retrieve the microphone, The Demon shoves him so hard the announcer falls down, and The Demon kicks him, or The Demon says, "You want this back, wimp? You want this back? Okay! Okay!" Then he wraps the cord around the man's neck and starts choking him. While The Demon laughs, the announcer sinks slowly to the floor, waving his arms and gasping for air. He looks into the TV camera and whines, "Please help me. Somebody help. Oh, my goodness. Let's just go to a commercial. I'll be back, fans. I hope."

In the middle of a match, The Masked Demon will turn toward the hissing, booing spectators who are shouting to the deaf, dumb and blind referee that The Demon has just thrown in the eyes of Cowboy Chuck Carlson or Big Dan Davis or Lucky Larry Jones some red powder meant to burn the eyeballs right out of their sockets; and The Demon hollers, "You better shut up! You better shut up!" One night in Odessa a skinny man with a switchblade jumped into the ring and tried to cut The Demon's tail off and ended up stabbing the referee in the thigh and getting his arm broken by a security guard, who seemed to enjoy doing it. Samson went to Hoffman afterward and said, "See what your ideas get."

Hoffman sat with his little fan blowing on his fat, red face and said, "Too bad it wasn't a televised match."

In Oklahoma City a stout, gray-haired woman squeezed herself through the ropes around the ring and tried to knee The Demon in his private parts.

For his first fourteen years as a professional wrestler, Samson was only one person: Samson The Strong Man, a good guy, and a world champion in the southwestern United States of America three times. He loved that wide championship belt made of leather and gold that the champions passed from one to another, changing hands at least once every three years. He loved it as if it had really meant something in the world of athletics, like an Olympic gold medal, and he supposed it did if people believed it did. He was proud because he knew he was good at what he did, even if it was just acting, and he always knew back then who he would be from one week to the next. Then he'd gone flabby; his face puffed up and made his eyes beady; the fans got tired of him. After Hoffman came on the scene, he told Samson that a change was overdue.

"Samson The Strong Man" was the name given him when he joined the circus in 1936. In between the circus and becoming a professional wrestler he went back to being Daryl Lee. He liked "Samson" better and preferred that people call him that or Sam or Sammy.

He left the circus in 1940 after he caught his wife with the clown. Leaving was part of his attempt to forget his marriage. He got a job in a gas station, but his second day, the owner told him to let the air out of people's tires while the gas was pumping, so they'd think they needed new ones or at least patch jobs. For a week he couldn't sleep. Then he went to the owner one morning, having worked himself into a red-hot frenzy, said, "I quit, you cheatin' bastard," and overturned a stack of oil cans, tore a brand new tire in half with his bare hands, walked down the road a few miles until his steam ran out, and then slept in a ditch for twenty hours, waking up in a rain storm, soaked, but feeling good about himself again.

He didn't have a steady job until after Pearl Harbor. In the Navy he met a Negro cook called King Kong Jones, who gave him the name of a pro wrestling promoter in Daryl Lee's home state of Texas.

No, he decides, the roles he plays as a professional wrestler are no excuse—that is all he is trying to do: make excuses. He is simply a son of a bitch.

Candy opens the bathroom door and stands naked in the harsh light, her eyes half closed, and she sleepily says, "I gotta trickle."

"I wanta be alone."

"I gotta trickle."

"Not now, woman."

"Sammy," she drones, "I gotta trickle real bad. You want me to trickle on your feet?"

"Do you have to talk like some goddamn kid?" Young women are all children: Lou Ann with her door slamming and shouting and Candy with her little-girl talk when she's sleepy. Dana Diane is the only real woman he knows.

"What's wrong, you big ole thing?" She puts her slim arms around his head, one of her nipples right under his nose, and he starts to get excited. But when she lays the side of her face on top of his head in a loving way, he yells, "Goddamn it! Watch the bruises!"

"You got these tonight? I didn't know he knocked you on your head." She separates the strands of his graying, thinning hair to see bruises made by a bronze ashtray. "You poor ole thing."

In his mind appears Lou Ann, scarlet-faced, mad as a hornet. He deserved it; he is sorry. But his ears and the back of his neck start burning with anger at Candy. "Quit, damn it!" In part, he doesn't want her looking at his bald spot and gray hairs. He knocks her hands away.

"Honey, I just—"

"Get out!"

"I gotta trickle!"

He stands up and stomps out, stops outside the door, turns, and what he says just comes out like vomit; he can't help himself. "Whore bitch!"

"What you call me?"

"Whore bitch."

"You know I ain't."

"You didn't hang around them wrestlin' contests for nothin'. I'm gonna ask Jake The Snake 'bout you. I can just see you with every wrestler. With every cowboy." Stars are popping and flashing everywhere, as if someone were taking pictures. Private eyes. "You, you and Kennedy. You and, and—"

She throws a big jar of face cream and hits him square in the nose. He staggers back, and she slams the bathroom door and locks it. As bad as Lou Ann.

He kicks it open, just to show her he can. She is backed against the bathtub, holding in front of her in one hand the razor she shaves her legs with. Her breasts are heaving. Her black eyes are flashing.

Damn, she looks good, naked and flushed, all fired up, the tendons in her pretty neck bulging, the muscles in her thighs taunt. He is about to melt. He wants to fall to his knees, crawl to her and beg forgiveness. Hug her legs and lick her pussy. But she suddenly bursts out with, "Who have *you* been screwin'?" And the razor rips the air.

Samson drives his fist into the wall, gets into some clothes, and for the second consecutive night, he is on the road.

THREE

Early in the morning Samson is in Donie, and in front of him on his mama's kitchen table are four fried eggs and six pancakes and a dozen buttermilk biscuits. Jars of jellies, sticks of margarine, and a cup of coffee.

"Eat," Mama says.

"I ain't hungry." He whispers because his sister is still asleep or pretending to be so that she won't have to see him. Poor Jean Marie, his twin sister (not identical), is a spinster, too huge for any man to handle. Six feet four and weighs more than Samson does. "What's Jean Marie doin' these days?"

"Same," says his mama, who is a tiny woman, not quite five feet. Deep liverish gouges underscore her eyes, and her wattled throat is a wreck of flesh. Her body is sinewy. "Same" means Jean Marie does nothing but keep the house clean, eat enough for six women, and watch game shows and soap operas on TV. Before she and Mama had a TV she read movie magazines and detective novels.

"I wish she didn't hate me," Samson says.

"Why, she don't hate you, Daryl Lee," his mama says as if she thinks he's crazy.

"She does and you should know it, Mama. It's because she thinks you think I'm some big success and she's nothin'. But she's really better than me. She's sweet and kind to you and was to Daddy and even to me when we was young. I'm just a fake. I ain't nothin'. I ain't no more than some clown. Listen, Mama. I been bad. I been bad a long time, and I'm gettin' worse."

This decision to confess all to his mama is reckless, he knows, but he hopes she will have some special wisdom that seventy years on earth have given her, some advice that will save him. And she will have the compassion and love to forgive him. After all, she is his mama.

"Those boys you wrestle really been beatin' up on you," she says, as though she just noticed, reaching an arm across the table, across the food she fixed, to touch his nose and the bruises on his forehead, inflicting pain with each touch.

In recent years his mama has become vain about her appearance and sits across from him now in a dark blue dress with a small flower pattern in it and white lace. Whenever he shows up unexpected, he has to wait in the living room while she puts on a Sunday dress and her silver wig and smears rouge on her cheeks. Only then will she come and hug him and kiss him, as if otherwise she is not worthy of receiving her guest, her own boy. Then she starts cooking whether he wants her to or not.

"Mama, I know you're proud of me, but you shouldn't be. You should be proud of Jean Marie."

"You're the boy. You're the one out there in the world makin' money and bein' famous."

"See. That's what I mean. That's why Jean Marie hates me and don't hardly ever comes out of her room when I'm here."

"I love your sister, you know that. She's a big help to me, but she ain't on TV, and she don't live in a big brick house in Houston, and she don't have no fine family."

"Oh, Mama." Samson wishes she wouldn't talk so loud. He cringes and looks over his shoulder at the doorway.

"You're a gifted athlete, Daryl Lee."

"It's all fake, Mama. I been tellin' you for years. I'm a fake."

"Don't look fake to me." She touches each of his bruises again.

"That hurts, Mama."

"See."

He looks around the room. The little house has not changed much in over thirty years, except for the TV set and the modern stove and refrigerator, all of which he paid for, gladly. At that very table he arm wrestled his daddy, starting at the age of four, his daddy using one finger to beat him. His daddy was six-six, had weighed three twenty-five when he died at the age of forty-six from a heart attack. Samson wonders if he will, too; is something in his genes ticking like a time bomb? He's almost there.

His daddy owned a grocery store in town, selling hardware as well, and cattle feed. Samson remembers being little and sitting on the wooden floor of the store and watching his daddy carry three one-hundred-pound sacks of feed at once out to a farmer's truck. Samson could do the same by the time he was twelve. When he was fourteen, he beat his daddy in arm wrestling.

Suddenly, sitting in this kitchen that has never been free of the smell of biscuits in Samson's lifetime, he wonders whether his daddy ever cheated on Mama. It is a stupid thought, he immediately tells himself. Daddy worked in the store fourteen hours a day and loved Mama with the devotion of a true Christian. They all went to church every Sunday and Wednesday to hear the soul-saving preaching of Reverend Fuller, whose pinch-faced wife and skinny, pale daughter sat in the front pew.

That poor skinny daughter had no friends. Kids (Daryl Lee, too, a couple of times) used to throw pebbles and clods of dirt at her on the school playground for no reason except that she was quiet and shy and frail and got top marks in spelling and that throwing things at her was kind of like throwing things at her daddy and, by extension, God, both of whom didn't seem to want anybody to have any fun.

Funny how things turned out. Fate. Destiny. God doing His job. That frail girl, his Dana Diane.

"How's the boys?" Mama asks.

"They're fine boys. Daryl Junior is almost a man."

"And Dana Diane?"

"She's a good wife." He pauses and looks at his big paws on the table, the fur on the back of them, the big cuticles, the big knuckles. "I don't deserve her. She's a brittle little woman. I worry 'bout her."

"You're a good husband, Daryl Lee. You're a good provider. A celebrity and all."

"Oh, Mama, you don't know how bad I am."

"You been bad?" It is Jean Marie who speaks. "Mama will never believe it." She has stopped in the doorway, blocking out any light coming from the living room, and there is no telling how long she has been there. Now she waddles across the kitchen floor, in a faded robe and old blue slippers. Samson starts to get up so he can hug her, but she says, "What ya gettin' up for?" and gives him a nasty look. "I just come in for my blood pressure pills." Her hair hangs to her shoulders, thin, oily, and the color of squash.

"How is your blood pressure?" he asks.

"The same."

"I could work you up a exercise program to help you lose weight."

"Sit down," Mama says to her.

She ignores Mama and glares at Samson's belly and smirks. "Heard you become The Devil," she says. "You never told us."

"It's just a new gimmick. You know how stupid all that stuff is. That promoter Hoffman, it was his idea."

"What's this about The Devil?" Mama asks.

"The Masked Demon, Mama. I'm called The Masked Demon in a lot of cities now. Hey, Jean Marie, how did you know?"

"Boyd Gleason at church was down in Houston and said he thought it was you but wasn't sure. He said you was real good, if it was you." She moves to the cabinet over the sink and reaches for a small plastic cylinder of pills.

"I don't believe it," Mama says.

"You look real good, Jean Marie," Samson says.

"She's gonna drop dead like your daddy if she don't watch out."

"Heck," Samson says and chuckles, "Jean Marie's fit as a fly. I'm the one's got to watch out."

"Nice seein' ya, Demon," Jean Marie says on her way

out. "I got things to do." Shuffling on her old slippers, which are starting to split at the sides. He'll buy a new pair and bring them next time, he decides.

"Oh, come on now. I don't hardly ever see you."

She flips up an arm and hand to say good-bye or "Go to hell," probably both.

When they were little, they swam together in the river, walked all over town holding hands, talked with each other about Mama and Daddy and God, helped each other with school work. He beat up four boys in third grade because they called her names. When she was thirteen she used to kiss his cheek every day and tell him he was the only person on earth she did not hate.

Now she is nasty to him, and it occurs to him that her nastiness is not merely jealousy showing itself. Maybe she sees through him, can look at him and sense a soul black with sin. She knows he is a demon.

"Oh, baby, I'm so proud," Mama says, not at all concerned about Jean Marie. She reaches across the table and touches the bright orange tie he put on at the Texaco station a block from her house. From the Texaco's pay phone he called a couple of florists to have them deliver flowers to Lou Ann and Candy. The recent fights with them are the worse they've ever had, or seem to be, and he fears finding an empty trailer in Oklahoma City and an empty house in Dallas.

"You don't listen, Mama. I need someone to talk to."

"You should be able to talk to Dana Diane."

"I can't I don't think."

"Why not?"

"Never mind."

"Don't you have friends, some of the boys you wrestle with?"

"Not really."

"I taught you to be friendly and make friends with people as long as they wasn't trash."

"Just let me talk, Mama. Please."

"Talk."

He stares at her. Is he crazy? His mama can't help him. She'll say, "I don't believe it," and ask him if he wants her to make some blueberry waffles.

"Talk."

"Damn it, Mama." He is trying not to cry.

"Don't cuss. It's trashy."

"I gotta go."

"Promise you won't cuss," she says, following him through the living room.

"Oh, hell, Mama."

"Promise."

"I gotta go." He turns and hugs her and kisses her old neck; then he hurries out of the house.

His mama stands on the porch of the white frame house that Samson recently paid to have painted, waving high in the air one of her thin arms, as he pulls his Cadillac out of the dirt driveway, raising a cloud of dust.

His and Dana Diane's house is an all brick with air conditioning, surrounded by shrubs and trees and other nice houses; their neighbors are lawyers and chiropractors and even a dentist three houses down, good people although they're snobs and won't wave back when he waves; they think he's a freak probably, a thought that makes his ears burn, but he likes the neighborhood and the house. It is a house he hopes will help his boys grow up to be happy and good.

When he gets home—this is truly home, here with Dana Diane and Benny Bob and Earl and Daryl Junior—he goes straight to bed, exhausted.

Despite all his worries he falls asleep immediately. He's too tired to think any more. But when he wakes up, he remembers dreaming about Hoffman; something blurry and wild happened in the dream, though he can't recall exactly what.

After his shower he goes downstairs to the kitchen, and

Dana Diane tells him that Hoffman called while he was sleeping. She's cutting up a frying chicken and doesn't look at him. He just stands staring at her back, then swallows hard and asks, "What he say?"

"Not much."

He watches her continue to mutilate the chicken. Is this the way she would react—not look at him and mutilate a chicken?

"He didn't say nothin'?"

"You need to call him."

He starts to think she knows nothing. Her not talking much, her not looking at him are an indication of nothing except seventeen years of marriage. After seventeen years you get used to a person. In seventeen years, Candy will be indifferent to his arrivals home. Nineteen seventy-nine. He will be sixty. Will he still be coming home? More likely he'll be dead.

"He wants me to call him?"

"Uh huh."

"He didn't say nothin' else?"

"Not really. Asked how I was. He was nice." And now that the chicken is all cut up, she turns to him and stretches up on her toes to kiss his cheek. She looks like a school teacher, Samson thinks, and she probably would have become one—an old maid school teacher cracking kids' knuckles—if he had not married her.

Turning from him and picking up a severed leg to roll in her special batter that makes her chicken so good, she says, "And, Daryl, we have a big problem."

"What?"

"Call Mr. Hoffman. Then we'll talk."

"Tell me now." The drumming of his heart fills his head.

"No. Call Mr. Hoffman first."

Samson climbs upstairs, his legs aching: too many bouts for too many years, too many women and not enough sleep. He sits on the edge of his and Dana Diane's bed and dials Hoffman's office.

"Hoffman, I hear you called my wife."

"Listen, Daryl. Everything's set for Mexico."

"You listen, Hoffman—" But he doesn't really have anything to say.

"I had a nice chat with your wife."

"Yeah?"

"She's a nice lady."

"What you tryin' to pull, Hoffman?"

"What do you mean? Listen, about Mexico. You'll get twenty more for each bout down there."

"What I got to do?"

"Come in next week on your way through Dallas, and we'll talk then. Sign the contracts and all."

Before Samson can say anything, Hoffman hangs up.

He goes into the bathroom and takes four aspirin and spends a few minutes dabbing hair-growing tonic on his head. Drinking this stuff would be a strange way of killing yourself, he thinks. Hair growing in your gut, on your tongue, in your throat. Then looking at his face in the mirror, he prays: "Please, God, don't ever let Dana Diane find out about what I been doin'. Please, God, I'll be good for now on. I'll change."

As he starts down the stairs, he imagines a scene in which he walks into the kitchen and says, "Well, honey, you wanted to talk." And Dana Diane says, "Talk? Talk about what?" God will make everything right. Then he imagines walking into the kitchen and saying, "Well, honey—" And Dana Diane turns around with the knife she was using on the chicken and rams it into his fat gut.

When he really does enter the kitchen, she turns to him, looking sad and resigned to something awful, and wipes her hands on a towel. She's been washing dishes. She needs a dishwasher.

"What is it, honey?"

"It's Daryl Junior."

"Daryl Junior?" Relief mixes with fear for his oldest boy.

"Yes. He, well, he got that little girlfriend of his—she's

going to have a baby." Her face shatters with grief, showing her age, and she cries.

"That little girl? What's her name? Jesus Christ."

"You don't need to swear."

"I didn't know she was more than fifteen."

"She isn't."

"I'll kill that boy."

"They're going to get married."

"Like hell."

"Saturday. They told me and her parents four days ago. I tried to call you at your motels, but they said you weren't in. Didn't you get any of my messages?"

Samson has long kept rented rooms in Oklahoma City and Dallas but never uses them anymore, of course. Dana Diane has never called him before. He usually calls her every few days. He steps forward and takes Dana Diane into his arms.

"You'll be here Saturday, won't you?"

"Yeah. But how are they gonna live?"

"They'll stay with us."

"He's only sixteen."

"I want him to finish school."

"Which means I not only feed his wife but I pay all the hospital bills, right?"

Samson looks around the shiny kitchen at the pine cabinets, the sink, the stove, the table, the big white refrigerator. He focuses on the refrigerator as if it were to blame for this mess; that goddamn refrigerator should have prevented this kind of thing.

As the afternoon wanes, Samson sits in his leather lounge chair in the living room with his littlest boys playing at his feet. There is still hope for them; if he changes, maybe they'll turn out all right; see, it is his fault, he has concluded, that Daryl Junior has done this awful thing. God is punishing him, Samson.

He can see into the kitchen where Dana Diane is fixing

supper, and he thinks about how stuffed with love his heart is for that frail woman and those boys. Why—if he loves this family so much—does he have Lou Ann and Candy? He feels an impulse to walk into the kitchen and tell Dana Diane how much he loves her and loves the way she has cooked and cleaned and cared for him and his boys all these years. But if he does that, won't he be a hypocrite? Won't he be a fake?

Dana Diane was everything he was looking for when he went back to Donie to visit Mama and Jean Marie after the war. He wanted a sweet Christian woman who could cook. No more phony blondes. No more smelly, lazy whores, like the ones he met while he was in the navy.

After all those years of being a faithful husband, what had happened to him? One thing, he did get lonely away from home in those hotel and motel rooms, always some sick pink or green or yellow color, never enough light, his having to listen to people in other rooms coughing and puking and laughing and screwing. And he didn't want just a whore; you could still be lonely as hell with a naked woman if she was a whore. Another reason was that maybe he wanted to be kind of born again, to start over, to be young again by starting another family. Well, that explained Lou Ann better than it did Candy, who was just something he missed when he was twenty. Then he shakes his head vehemently.

"Why you shakin' your head?" Earl, the nine-year-old, asks. He gets no answer.

No, she isn't just something he missed when he was twenty. After all, there was the lion girl (she had a fine body and a way of—); he loves Candy, loves her deeply; it is not just her ways in bed that have a hold on him.

He tries to think of other explanations for turning bad. Of course a man got tired of his wife's body after so many years. Earl is standing between Samson's legs, his hands on Samson's knees, saying, "Daddy, Daddy." Samson is staring into the kitchen at his wife. He is tired of her in bed maybe, but he is certain he loves her more now than ever. Earl is frail like Dana Diane. "Why are you movin' your head like that?"

"Huh?"

"Like this." The child shakes his head furiously, then nods furiously.

"I was just thinkin'."

Benny Bob has been sneaking up on Earl. Although he is two years younger than Earl, he is bigger, has his daddy's frame. He has a Mohawk haircut and for two years now has been saying he will grow up to be a wrestler. He is going to be Big Indian Ben and scalp his opponents. Benny Bob throws Earl to the floor and gets on top of him and grabs his hair. Earl screams.

While the boys wrestle, Samson looks again in the direction of the kitchen. Dana Diane is turning over the popping, sizzling chicken. He keeps staring at her while Benny Bob hits Earl on the head with a rubber tomahawk. Dana Diane has the scrawniest butt, Samson thinks. He used to joke about it when he was drinking with a bunch of men or playing poker or working out with weights in a gym; he'd say she was built like the cartoon character Gumby, flat in front and flat in back. He doesn't joke about it anymore. That scrawny butt makes him kind of sad for some reason. Then he thinks about Candy's smooth, round bottom. He hates himself for loving her butt. In a few seconds, though, he starts hating Dana Diane for having a scrawny butt. Earl is crying, "Dad! Make him stop!" Benny Bob is hooting like an Indian on the warpath. Then Samson hates Candy for having that awfully fine bottom. Whose fault is it that he's a son of a bitch? And what about Lou Ann's butt? In her case it's more her big tits that are the issue.

"Dad! Make him stop!"

All of a sudden, damn it, if he isn't getting excited right here with all these thoughts of tits and butts—and his littlest boys playing at his feet.

"Dad!"

"Goddamn it, go play somewhere else!" The boys stop struggling and stare at him. "Go on. Get the hell out of here before I whip both your behinds."

They run out of the room and out the front door. They must be scared to run like that. Running off to get girls pregnant. What can you expect from boys with a father like him.

Dana Diane looks in to see what the trouble is, and he is furious with love and pity and hate for her. He has to get out.

FOUR

Samson is in the locker room at the arena when Daryl Junior walks in, surprising him. Daryl Junior's hair is black, brushed back like Elvis Presley's. He's about five-six, Samson estimates, and weighs around one forty, another child in whom Samson's genes have lost out. He has come down to the arena with his girl, Mary Ann, and Samson goes out into the hallway to see her. He can't look at her, at them, and think of her as his son's fiancée; it's a funny French word that has always sounded a little obscene anyway, like most French words.

Mary Ann's hair and eyebrows are pale yellow. She wears no make-up. A shy, skinny girl. Her eyes are brownish-gray. Almost no hips—how in the world will a baby live and grow in that tiny space? She is wearing a white dress with small pink flowers all over it, her calves pencils, her knees knobby; she looks like the little-girl virgin she should be.

As Samson and Mary Ann smile and avoid each other's eyes and try to think of something to say, Daryl Junior says, "Ben and Earl said you stomped out of the house and didn't even eat supper."

He *had* to leave. He walked the streets around the arena where drunks sprawled against old buildings.

"Yeah, I, ah, had to—I all of a sudden—" Then he realizes he doesn't need to make excuses, to explain his actions to his son. Good God, the boy is the one who should be explaining a few things.

"I figured you got mad after Mom told you about me and Mary Ann."

"Your mama says you're gettin' married Saturday."

Mary Ann's face turns almost purple, an unhealthy color, and Samson wonders whether she's sick.

"I'd like to meet your mama and daddy some time."

"Yes, sir." Her voice is fragile, glasses tinkling as you touch them together.

"You'll *meet* them Saturday," Daryl Junior says as if his daddy is a moron.

Samson still hopes something will happen to fix everything; God will make everything right.

Daryl Junior is saying he doesn't think he'll stay in school.

"I think it'd be a good idea to stay."

"I thought maybe I'd work on cars."

Samson nods his head. His boy a grease monkey. No college now. Samson's fault: sinful, weak, never home. God is punishing him through his boy. Samson remembers a little boy who stole from Daddy's store. His mother died of cancer, and the boy blamed himself because he was a thief. Became a drunk before he was twenty.

The wrath of God.

Mary Ann is looking at her feet. His daughter-in-law. He is going to be a granddaddy—he hadn't really realized it until just now. A bit of warmth flows into his heart through a valve that just now opens a little.

"Want a cigarette?"

Samson is startled to see his son holding a cigarette out to him. The boy knows his daddy doesn't smoke. In the other hand, hanging at his side, is a pack of Camels. Hoffman's brand.

"When you start smokin'?"

"While back."

The boy is showing off. For him? For the girl? "You know

I don't smoke, boy," he says sternly.

Daryl Junior shrugs, puts his pack of Camels back in his shirt pocket, and smiles at Mary Ann, who frowns.

Good Lord, his boy is smoking and screwing.

"Mary Ann's never seen you wrestle."

"That why you come down here?"

"That and to see just how mad you are."

Samson's opponent in tonight's match, Tonga, walks past. "Hey, Ray," Samson says. "How you feelin'?"

"Man, you can just put a sleeper hold on me in the first minute far as I'm concerned." Tonga weighs four hundred pounds. Everybody has to back up against the wall to let him get past.

"So how mad are you, Dad?" Daryl Junior asks.

"I ain't mad."

"Shit, Dad. I know you are."

Cussing, too.

In a Texas Cage Death Match, the opponents fight inside a ring around which high walls of wire caging have been constructed. The match, having no time limit, ends when one wrestler is unconscious and has to be carried off on a stretcher, his face usually smeared with watery, tasteless blood.

Samson The Strong Man's opponent, Tonga The African Wild Man, has yellow stripes painted on his face. On his womanly tits are red X's, and down the center of his huge belly, twice as big as Samson's, is a thick vertical line of green. This massive black man who's so big he can hardly move wears nothing but a loincloth. The wild thing about him is the piercing screams he lets out, the sounds of a lower order of life; the sounds, the TV announcer says, of a non-Christian and a cannibal.

Before the bout begins, Samson and Tonga glare at each other from opposite corners of the enclosed ring, the one waving the jawbone of an ass, the other a spear. These weapons are taken away by the referee. The opponents then wave their fists. Samson The Strong Man shouts, "You gonna pay, Wild Man, for what you done to Buffalo Bill Branson." The fans who are up on the happenings in Southwestern World Championship Wrestling send up a bloodthirsty cheer.

Buffalo Bill makes a timely entrance in a wheelchair, coming down the aisle leading to Samson's corner. Bill is wearing a neck brace and sunglasses as if he were a blind man. Tonga yells, "Ou ga buga bu!" and lets out a mad scream. He waddles as fast as he can over to the side where Bill sits and puts his fingers through the wires of the cage and makes obscene noises to indicate he wants to finish Buffalo Bill off. But he's caged, of course, and Samson The Strong Man grabs him by the shoulders and throws him to the canvas. The bout has begun. The bell rings belatedly.

For most of the match, Samson is backed against the ropes, getting whipped pretty badly, while the crowd of cowboys and winos and fat women and retarded-looking kids scream for Tonga's blood.

Samson's mind is not on his job. Twice his timing is off, and he gets clipped by punches. He's working on a plan. He can join the Big Time Wrestling Association in Michigan. He was offered a job there by the promoters in 1955. If they still want him, there will be no more putting up with Hoffman. He will move Dana Diane and the boys and Mary Ann and his grandbaby up there to Detroit. But as soon as he thinks the word "Detroit," he sees smokestacks and suet-blackened skyscrapers. Snow drifts twenty feet high. Gray skys every day. Rude cops. He has heard that the meanest people on earth live up there. In contrast, Texas towns are friendly and blue-skied, safe.

And what about Candy and Lou Ann? Could he abandon them? He could send them money in envelopes with no return address. But he imagines both of them riding up to his house in Detroit in Hoffman's car, getting out and going for his eyes with their fingernails, Hoffman laughing his head off, Dana Diane having a heart attack, Daryl Junior sucking on a Camel and blowing smoke in his daddy's face.

Samson sighs, not even knowing that Tonga has put a rip in his Samson The Strong Man outfit, a yellow thing that is supposed to be the skin of a lion.

He doesn't hear the shouts and jeers of the crowd or feel the pain in his lips and gums where he's been punched. He's just letting himself be tossed around by Tonga.

He is thinking about all the people he loves—his boys, Dana Diane, Mama, Jean Marie, Candy, Lou Ann, Tina Lee, and that baby inside Lou Ann. Also squeezed into his heart is his grandbaby. His heart is bursting.

He reckons he'll have to do the bouts in Mexico. Screw sheep or pigs. Whatever Hoffman has in mind.

"Make a show of it," Tonga keeps muttering. "It's 'bout time you cleaned my greens."

Samson leans into a punch that sends him down, for real. Tonga thinks he's going to mess his loincloth.

"Get up, get up," Tonga hisses from the corner of his mouth, as he waddles around the cage with his arms raised like a victor. "Get up, you son of a bitch, and clean my greens."

The referee stands over Samson but hasn't started the count yet. He looks around for help. With his eyes he pleads with Buffalo Bill Branson to help him, but Bill shrugs his shoulders. Then Tonga throws himself on Samson as if he wants to eat him, giving the referee an excuse for not counting. The referee starts hopping around, yelling, "Break! Break!" Tonga knocks him down, and the referee, with much relief, lies unconscious.

Samson opens his eyes slowly. He sees the blurry face of a crazy-looking colored boy. He sees white teeth and a glitter of gold. "Get up and clean my greens, man."

Samson is thinking about all the women and all the children and the mama he loves. Their images float in front of him along with the sweaty, contorted, painted face of the fat colored boy. "I love you."

"What?" Tonga says.

Then Samson understands. The fans are screaming. He has a job to do. He has three families to support. Quickly, he is up, behind Tonga, and has his arms wrapped around Tonga's chest, still thinking about all the people he loves, knowing he isn't going to be able to stop loving anybody, isn't going to be able to change too fast, maybe never. It will go on. He will be sixty, and Candy will be there in Dallas, his wife. Yes, his wife. Lou Ann in Oklahoma City. More children will come, and he will love them. Grandchildren, too. He will do hideous things in Mexico to save it all. He feels like crying. He just *has* to buy Dana Diane a dishwasher.

He hears the fans yelling, "Kill him! Kill him!" And he squeezes Tonga and calls, "Oh, Jesus!" as if he were Bible Bob.

God will continue to punish him if he does not change.

"Oh, Jesus," he groans, his heart bursting.

"Oh, my Jesus," he mutters, as he crushes Tonga in his famous bear hug.

DEJA VU

B renda is lying on the bed in her room with the door shut, but she can hear the TV in the living room. Explosions and gunfire. Dana and Kirk are watching *The Terminator* on cable. They always watch TV here rather than at his apartment. Kirk was bad about paying his cable bill, so Telecable disconnected him. Brenda is in her room because she and Dana had a fight before Kirk came over. It was about him, and Brenda ended up calling Dana a fool.

Brenda looks up at the cracks in the ceiling and thinks she can make out the face of a demon, the way some people can hear satanic lyrics when they play a record backwards. She knows Dana will spend the night at Kirk's and doesn't cherish the thought because the last two Friday nights a couple of teenage boys have climbed onto the roof, stomped around, and scared her out of her wits. The noise, Brenda thought, sounded like something that went along with devastating violence; the first time, she thought a tree had fallen on the house or a plane had crashed or an earthquake had hit. Dana was terrified, too, for a few minutes, but then said kids did stupid things all the time and didn't mean any harm.

"How you know they didn't? Maybe they were looking for a way in," Brenda said. She had looked out a window and had seen them running away down the street, two lanky figures eerie under the street lights, their windbreakers billowing out behind them like capes.

"They're not going to try to get in when it's obvious we're home." Dana and Brenda had both been still up and had lights on all over the house and the TV turned up. Kirk wasn't there because he was doing the inventory at K-Mart.

"Maybe *we* were what they wanted," Brenda said.

"Kids do lots of things that don't make sense. Sue at work said her twelve-year-old tried to burn up the front yard so he wouldn't have to mow the grass."

"I think they're on drugs."

"You wanta call the police?"

"All kids are on drugs now days."

"Want *me* to call the police? They'll come here and ask a bunch of questions and then not do a damn thing. I know. I used to call them on Ed, that first guy I lived with."

Brenda shook her head.

But the second time, she was alone when it happened, and she did call. The policeman was polite but seemed bored. Brenda saw the neighbors standing in their doorways and in front of their windows, pointing at her and Dana's house and at the police car.

"Do you know the boys' names, Miss?" the policeman asked. "Do you know where they live?"

Brenda shook her head.

"You say you didn't get a good look at them because it was dark?" The policeman was tall and young, maybe twenty-one. "You ever have trouble with peeping toms, Miss?"

"They can't see anything by getting on the roof."

The policeman shrugged.

Dana knocks on Brenda's door and says, "We're going. I don't know when I'll be home."

Brenda can tell from Dana's voice that she's still angry. "Okay." Then Brenda says, "Bye."

She hears them murmuring, then hears the front door shut. Bells hang from the doorknob and make a lot of noise. When Brenda goes into the living room, she finds Coke cans and an open bag of pretzels on the coffee table she bought at a flea market and refinished a few months ago, just after she and Dana bought the house.

They both used to work the day shift at a 7-Eleven convenience store, and one day they started telling each other how sick they were of landlords raising their rents and never fixing anything.

Dana's landlord was always dropping in and saying he had a right to inspect his property and saying, "I want to remind you I don't tolerate any immoral behavior on my property." Then he'd grin and say, "Unless, of course, I'm a party involved in it." He was fat and had the biggest forearms Dana had ever seen. She told Brenda she was afraid he'd grab her wrists, and there would be no way she could get loose.

So Brenda and Dana bought this house together for thirty thousand dollars. It was all they could afford, although Dana quit her job at the 7-Eleven and started working at the Zenith factory for twice as much an hour. Brenda warned her she'd get laid off a lot, but Dana said she wasn't worried and went out and bought an almost-new Firebird.

Brenda has a Corvette. Even though it was four years old when she bought it, the payments are high. But she saves money by working on it herself. Knowing how to change the oil, spark plugs, wires, and belts and how to do most repairs makes her proud. Her ex-husband, Gus, taught her a few things, but she learned other things on her own from books. She learned that some of the things Gus told her were wrong.

She also knows more about cars than Kirk does. He's twenty-two, six years younger than both Brenda and Dana. He works in the stockroom at K-Mart. He's tall and lean—his jeans are always baggy in the butt—and Brenda admits he's kind of good looking with a strong jaw and a straight nose. Dana has a puffy-looking face and a weak chin, but a good figure, a small waist and full breasts. (Brenda considers herself prettier but knows she could lose ten, maybe fifteen, pounds.)

Even though Kirk's good looking, Brenda doesn't know why Dana goes out with him. She thinks Dana's getting too serious and is going to get hurt for sure. When they bought the house together, Brenda and Dana agreed that men were no longer a major part of their lives. Dana had lived with two men. The first one beat her; the second had "gone nuts," Dana said, and started giving all his money to TV evangelists. Dana and Brenda joked that they might occasionally "use" a man but that one would never come between their partnership (as co-owners of a house) or their friendship.

Now, for the last seven weeks, Dana has spent most of her free time with Kirk and has him over at the house a lot. "I don't have any privacy anymore," Brenda said during their fight this evening. "Every time I step out of the shower I'm afraid Kirk's going to be there spying on me."

"I don't think," Dana said, "that Kirk is interested in seeing you naked."

"I didn't mean that. He's just always here."

A few days ago, he asked Brenda if she'd work on his Camaro for him. It has rear tires that look ten times too big. The car is rusty and beat up. There's always bird shit on it, also. Brenda would never go out with a man who had bird shit on his car. On his rear bumper, Kirk has a sticker that says, "Want to get laid? Crawl up the ass of a chicken. Then wait."

Gus doesn't anymore, but he used to like bumper stickers. Plastered on the back of the old Falcon he drove when he and Brenda were married were three: "Eat your heart out. I'm married"; "My other car's a Rolls Royce"; and "Dentists do it with precision."

Gus wanted to be a dentist and was going to college when Brenda married him, but he flunked out his senior year. Brenda couldn't believe it. For their first anniversary she'd even had some stationery printed—to use in the future; at the top of each sheet of paper was "Dr. and Mrs. Gus Harris." She thought the stationery would inspire him to study harder. But he already studied; certain things just wouldn't stick in his brain. Now he drives a UPS truck.

After the divorce, Brenda lived with a Volvo salesman for nearly a year. Then he came home one night and said he was going to marry another woman.

After she watches the CNN news for half an hour, Brenda goes into the kitchen and washes the dishes. Dana never has time anymore. Dana used to help out with everything—mowing the grass, dusting, mopping—and she and Brenda used to spend their evenings together, eating popcorn and watching TV.

The pipes groan when she runs water, and once she thinks she hears a noise on the roof. But when she shuts off the faucet, she hears nothing but water dripping under the house.

The old widow lady who lives across the street with three cats and two dogs recently told her that the crime rate in the neighborhood has always been high—a lot of burglaries and vandalism (smashed car windows and paint splashed on the sides of people's houses).

When she and Dana first looked at the house, Brenda thought the neighborhood looked a little run down, but she loved the house itself. It was small and old, but it had character. She loved the wide strips of woodwork bordering the doors and running across the tops of walls. She loved the old bathroom fixtures and the wooden toilet-paper holder. After they lived in the house for a month, they found out they needed a new furnace. All the faucets leak, and the lights flicker and dim whenever Dana or Brenda turns on the clothes dryer or the window air conditioner. Brenda often stares into the fuse box at the switches and fuses—as if she could tell whether the house is on the verge of going up in the flames of an electrical fire.

She has fallen out of love with the house, the way she fell out of love with Gus and a dozen other men and boys in her life.

While they argued this evening, Dana finally brought up Gus. She said, "You act like you're my mother or something. Besides, who are you to talk? You and your weird love affair with your ex-husband."

But it's not a love affair—not in Brenda's mind. It's true that she occasionally sees Gus, but she hasn't loved him for a long time. When he's drunk, he calls and tells her he misses her, and sometimes she lets him come over. She likes the passionate, playful way he makes love to her. They drink beer and kid each other about the fat they're putting on. She pats his thinning hair. Then Gus usually ruins it by saying he loves her and wants to marry her again—and worst, wants to take care of her.

"Nobody's taking care of me," Brenda always says. "Not again. I take care of myself."

But sometimes, when she wakes up in the morning with him holding her, she's tempted.

Close to midnight, Brenda is lying in bed, reading *Gone with the Wind*. Last month Gus took her to see the movie. She'd never seen it before. For the last couple of weeks she's been reading a few pages of the novel when she gets time and isn't tired. Suddenly, there are heavy footsteps on the roof. She drops her book and looks up at the cracks in the ceiling, that demon face. Then she gets out of bed, just to stand in the middle of the room. She's wearing a nightgown and wishes she were dressed.

The boys seem to be racing back and forth on the rear

section of the roof, which has almost no slope. They're right over her room. She yells, "Get off!" The noise stops for a moment, then starts again. "I've got a gun!" She hopes they believe her, but they now seem to be jumping up and down. "Why are you doing this?" One of the boys taps out a rhythm as if he's dancing.

She looks around the room, but she doesn't know for what. Then she feels she has to get out of the house. She hates this damn house. If she doesn't get out, something horrible will happen. She picks up a photo album that contains pictures of herself and her parents, as if she were saving it from a fire. She runs to the living room but doesn't fling open the front door as she imagined she would. The noise has stopped. She stands still for several minutes, clutching her album to her chest, listening. Then she looks out windows, seeing no one.

Silence. She starts wandering through the house, too agitated to sit. "The bastards. The little bastards," she says. She's startled when the guy next door starts his motorcycle. After he roars off, it's quiet again. And she starts to cry.

The way she feels is familiar: she is somewhere she's been before. Was it the night she told Gus she wanted a divorce? No. It's like the morning she woke up, realizing she wanted the divorce. She got up that morning, made tea, walked around their apartment, then went back to the bedroom and looked at Gus, who was still asleep, his hair a mess, his mouth hanging open exposing a couple of teeth that had big cavities.

She had thought she would love him forever. In a similar way, she thought that she and Dana would be happy together, that when she and Dana bought his house together life was finally "working out."

The phone rings. She's certain it's Gus. Drunk again, calling to say he misses her, wanting to come over. She lets the phone ring until it stops, but she knows he will call back in a minute. She quickly decides she'll answer, and she'll let him come over. But she'll make him get out before morning; she won't let him sleep here, holding her. And tomorrow she'll think about really getting a gun. Or at least a dog.

The author

Mark Spencer was raised in the Ohio River Valley. His first collection of stories *Spying on Lovers* won the 1988 Patrick T.T. Bradshaw Book Award. Spencer is married and lives in Lawton, Oklahoma. He is at work on a new novel titled *The Bomb Shelter.*